Sleepless Days

Sleepless Days

Translated by Leila Vennewitz

Jurek Becker

HBJ

A Harvest/HBJ Book
A Helen and Kurt Wolff Book

Harcourt Brace Jovanovich, Publishers
San Diego   New York   London

Requests for permission to make copies of any
part of the work should be mailed to:
Permissions, Harcourt Brace Jovanovich, Publishers,
Orlando, Florida 32887.

LIBRARY OF CONGRESS CATALOGING IN PUBLICATION DATA
Becker, Jurek, 1937–
   Sleepless days.
   Translation of Schlaflose Tage.
   "A Helen and Kurt Wolff book."
   I. Title.
PZ4.B3952S1   [PT2662.E294]   833'.9'14   79-1811
ISBN 0-15-182982-9
ISBN 0-15-682765-4 (Harvest/HBJ : pbk.)

Printed in the United States of America
First Harvest/HBJ edition 1986
A B C D E F G H I J

Translator's Acknowledgment

To my husband, William, I am deeply grateful

for his continuing advice and assistance

throughout the translation of this book.

Leila Vennewitz

Sleepless Days

A few weeks after

his thirty-sixth birthday, while giving a lesson which until that moment had proceeded without incident, Simrock for the first time in his life became aware of his heart. It was a terrible shock, and he broke off a sentence at such an inappropriate point that many of the youngsters suspected a joke and laughed out of politeness. Yet the pain was not great; it was more like a gentle pressure, a suggestion of a pain that, had he felt it in any other part of his body, would have gone almost unnoticed. In this case, however, Simrock felt like someone plunging from glowing health into illness. He gripped his chair and waited.

The students soon quieted down, even the less observant realizing that something was wrong with their teacher. Only one girl, wishing to complete the interrupted sentence, persisted in holding up her arm.

Simrock told his students he wasn't feeling well and that they were to occupy themselves as they thought best, but quietly. Then he told the secretary he was going home and left the building. When one of his colleagues asked him in the corridor whether anything was the matter, he replied, with a smile now: "Nothing serious, just the old pump."

He walked into the nearby park and sat down on the grass. Although there were several signs saying KEEP OFF THE GRASS, he knew from previous visits, and now observed again, that people did not take these signs very seriously. He preferred the grass to one of the many unoccupied benches, you couldn't fall off the grass; besides, he could lie down without worrying that he might be taken for a drunk or a vagrant.

Health, Simrock told himself, was not nearly so important for happiness as illness was for unhappiness, and he was unhappy. And in one so young, too, he thought. With the aid of his wristwatch he took his pulse and counted seventy-one beats to the minute. Then it occurred to him that he had no idea what to do with this figure; the last time he had taken his pulse was as a child, seventy-one beats could just as well be alarming as perfectly normal. It was to Simrock's regret that his emotions frequently led to actions whose significance was already unclear to him a few minutes later. He had known this weakness of his for a long time and sometimes suffered from it, but at the moment there were more important things to think about, his heart needed to see a doctor. The trouble was that he didn't care to place his life in the hands of the amiable bungler who invariably and without question prescribed whatever tablets he asked for; he didn't even expect the young man to offer any worthwhile suggestions. Simrock would have loved to know a doctor the way he knew his wine merchant, who brought out special wines for him from under the counter, French or unsugared

Baden wines that as an ordinary customer he would never have been shown. To be treated by a doctor under the counter, he thought: the idea amused him.

He stretched himself out and held up one hand against the sun, which was too bright even for his closed eyes. He thought it was a good sign that his heart was behaving quietly, although he was monitoring it. When, after a short while, he opened his eyes, he found himself looking into the face of a dog. For a few seconds he felt his heart pounding, but, he immediately reassured himself, even a healthy heart would have reacted similarly to a shock of that kind. The shrill voice of an old woman shouted: "Stop that!" whereupon the dog ran off as if it had just remembered something extremely important. Simrock had never watched a dog run from so low a level, the movements looked funny to him. He then proceeded to try to recall all the people who to his knowledge had heart trouble. Under his breath he recited the names of his relatives and friends, in alphabetical order, then combed the city from north to south, district by district, determined to omit no one. Possibly, he hoped, there was advice to be had here or there, vital information, for as a novice he was dependent on the experience of veteran invalids. He might even be able to find out which was the best clinic to go to and which was the best doctor to avoid. Yet however systematically he went about it, all he could remember was the names of people who had died. He thought: My God, it's all too much. He told himself he really shouldn't give up yet, then thought: Perhaps I'm exaggerating. It seemed quite understandable to exaggerate in his situation; indeed, he saw his only hope in the fact that he might be exaggerating. After the first shock, he reasoned, he might see his way clear to go on living. Then he fell asleep and did not wake up until the noise of the kids going home from school spread through the park.

*

Simrock's wife, Ruth, had to laugh when, after telling her all about it, he went as far as to claim that the incident signified a turning point in his own life and thus also in hers and would presumably have consequences that at present he could not foresee. She shook her head a few times, making him wonder whether her response was going to consist entirely of wordless headshaking. Then she asked him: "Would you like to know how often I have had a pain in my chest? Fifty times at least. And real pain, not just the way you describe it. The first time just after Leonie was born, and since then it has acted up again and again. But did you ever hear me say as much as a single word?"

Simrock said: "In case you think I'm grateful to you for sparing me your worries, you're mistaken. I don't feel spared, I feel excluded, perhaps even deceived."

He knew this was exaggerated, but it sounded pretty good. He thought: It's true, though, that her chest pains would have scared me more yesterday.

Ruth said: "I didn't mean to accuse you of lacking concern for me. I just wanted to reassure you. I wanted to show you that your heart attack is really something quite trivial which you don't have to get into a panic about. Unless you intend to make a fool of yourself."

Simrock thought: Even if she's right, she must know that she shouldn't put it that way. She's expecting me to contradict her, not to see it her way.

He said: "I'll give some thought to whether or not I want to make a fool of myself. I haven't made up my mind yet."

Ruth looked at him seriously for a few seconds, then left the room. Simrock thought: That's how one word leads to another. He sat on the sofa, motionless and uncomfortable, but no longer on account of his heart: it was a discomfort that only the absence of happiness could explain. This condition was not new to him; he was often seized by a discontent that he considered unproductive because, instead of making him face up to its causes, it invariably turned into self-pity. If now and then he accused himself of being a weakling, he tried to rationalize this by telling himself that he was a person who lacked ambition, that he simply wasn't interested in tugging at every little chain he discovered around his wrists or ankles. Discontent over these shackles, he would reason, was presumably less irksome than the effort to rebel.

Ruth called from the kitchen: "D'you want peppermint tea or cocoa?"

Simrock went into his daughter's room. Leonie was lying under the table, over which she had draped blankets to turn it into a cave. Only her head was sticking out of a gap; on the rug in front of her lay a book from which she pointedly refrained from looking up. Simrock stood around indecisively, anxious to start a conversation but at a loss for a subject. With his mouth already open to make a remark that even he regarded as unnecessary, he remembered how irritated he sometimes was when Leonie interrupted his own reading with idle comments. He then realized what a relief it was not to have to carry on a conversation right now. He became aware that he had gone into Leonie's room not out of a desire for a conversation, or from absent-mindedness, but, rather, with the intention of discharging his responsibilities toward the child, the way one goes to one's job, to perform one's duty. His task was: first, to stifle any feeling of isolation; second, to satisfy the child's thirst for security; finally, to be the person available for any form of communication. He told himself that on a day like today he could very well do without all that.

Leonie asked: "What does 'homogeneous' mean?"

Simrock explained it at too great a length, and she was

already deep in her book again before he had brought his little ship into port. He knelt down, stroked her head, and asked: "What are you reading?"

Without raising her eyes from the book, she lifted it slightly to allow him to read the title on the cover for himself. Ruth called from the kitchen: "Well, what's it to be— peppermint tea or cocoa?"

Later he lay in bed while Ruth was still busy with chores outside the room. Most evenings he helped her dispose of the daily pile of dirty dishes, but tonight he had asked to be excused on account of his condition. The bedside radio was turned on, but Simrock was not listening; he was trying to concentrate on a certain thought. After a few minutes he found he wasn't succeeding. Suddenly he couldn't even remember the subject with which the thought he had just been trying to concentrate on was connected, not even vaguely. He couldn't think clearly, there were so many things mixed up in his head; individual words emerged briefly from the tangle, only to disappear again before he could place them in any kind of order.

So he might as well listen to the voices coming from the radio. A man was interviewing a woman who, to judge by her voice, was about fifty. The woman was describing how she went shopping twice a week, and how the store clerks, who by this time all knew her, were invariably helpful and pleasant and, above all, honest. She could only recall a single instance during her three years in this area when the money taken from her had exceeded the value of the goods, and even there she felt it might well have been an error. Simrock thought: What trite stuff we're getting on the air these days. The woman went on to describe a coffee party she enjoyed going to every Thursday, one week at the home of one friend, the next at another's, everyone taking turns. Suddenly Simrock saw the point of the whole thing: the woman was blind. From then on he listened with greater interest, finding it agreeable that the woman should discuss her situation so calmly and without self-pity.

The interviewer asked if she would care to tell them something about her dreams. The woman said she could hardly remember anything of her very early days. If the accident had occurred when she was twenty or even thirty, things might be different. But as it was, her life as a sighted person lay so far in the past that the few remaining memories no longer influenced her dreams. To be specific: even in her dreams she was blind. Her dreams consisted of hearing, touching, smelling—in other words, of the same sensory perceptions to which she was exposed when awake, and never of colors, which she assumed was the point of his question. The interviewer asked whether she had any idea at all of the concept of color. Yes, the woman said, she did, she knew that colors had to do with the nature of surfaces but she was incapable of imagining any particular color. Scarlet, lime-green, purple were empty words for her, words she employed while flying blind, so to speak, the only exception being the color black. She had once been asked whether she didn't regret having no more memory of vision. After giving it a lot of thought she had replied: No, if anything she was glad. If there were any hope of her regaining her sight, her answer would undoubtedly have been different. As things were, however, she felt that the longing for a condition that, although it could be dreamed about, could not be approached even to the smallest degree, would merely hamper a person in the task, which was difficult enough anyway, of coming to terms with the situation. And the memory of sight was, after all, the same thing as the longing for it.

Simrock was moved, his eyes filled with tears, and then again after he had wiped away the first ones. When the next program had begun, he was surprised at having been so moved, for he didn't think this would have been his normal reaction. He told himself that his emotion could not have been produced by the blind woman alone, that she might have triggered it but not caused it; no, the reason for his emotion must be sought in his own situation. He tried to imagine how differently he would have reacted to such a radio program even yesterday, but again his thoughts became so confused that, in spite of every effort of will, he could not place them in any reasonable order.

Then he was awakened by the sounds Ruth made as she undressed. A slipper dropping on the floor, her watch being placed with a hard click on the bedside table, a chair being shifted. The draft made by her turning back her quilt. Simrock knew that all this was done deliberately but also that she did not mean to be inconsiderate. He thought: How silly of me, I should have asked her to let me sleep today.

The bedroom was the most cheerful room in the apartment. For the first four years of their marriage they had had to live in a single room, three and a half of those years with Leonie, and they had looked forward with so much pleasure to having their own bedroom that, long before they possessed it, they had devised a set of bedroom rules just for the sake of filling their minds with something related to their future happiness. These rules were still in force today, and they had seldom been ignored in the past. Rule One stated that outside quarrels ceased to count in this room. Both knew all ten rules by heart, and whenever one of them observed an infraction on the part of the other, it was only necessary to call out the appropriate number to pull the offender up short. At least this was normally the case. Sometimes, especially in the early days, they had felt a bit foolish. But since, during even the most violent quarrel, no doubts had ever been raised as to the value of the rules, they were still living off the little capital that they had invested many years before—to their advantage, in Simrock's opinion—although in quite different circumstances. Inside this room the tone of their voices was not to be compared with that of outside. The moment they passed through the door it was as if they cast off their irritation like a superfluous garment; and even if next day one of them tried to cling to his anger at the other, a perceptible change had taken place: because of the intervening night, that anger was no longer what it had been before. The blaze had lost some of its heat, and it was necessary to look for better justification.

Simrock pretended to be asleep while having no choice but to follow Ruth's movements and activities behind his back. When he heard her swallowing her pill with a mouthful of water and then setting down the glass with unnecessary emphasis, he thought: I wouldn't put it past her to crawl under my quilt after all that's happened. Then, after more than a minute had passed, he thought: Let's hope she comes soon, so we can get it over with.

He had to wait for a maddeningly long time before Ruth touched his shoulder and asked why he was pretending to be asleep. He did not respond, although he was fully aware that there was nothing to be gained through silence. Raising her voice, she followed with: "Listen, I asked you a question."

Simrock turned around toward her, doing his best to look half asleep. He said: "How's anybody supposed to sleep with all that racket?"

Ruth did not insist on a proper answer. Quickly, as if now she couldn't put it off any longer, she slipped in beside Simrock, snuggled up to him, and closed her eyes. As he looked at her, Simrock admitted to himself that even now he did not find her proximity unpleasant, but he said: "Not tonight, please, if you don't mind."

He kissed her forehead with ostentatious affection. After all, he told himself, there was nothing in the bedroom rules about being a helpless prey to the carnal desires of the other. On the contrary, Rule Four made it clear that absence of desire was sufficient reason for refusal and no cause for reproach. Absence of desire, according to their theory, was not to be explained solely in terms of free will on the part of the person experiencing it: it also had to be looked at in relation to the partner. At the time, of course, they had been convinced that this was more of an academic problem, included for the sake of completeness, than a problem that might assume practical significance in their life together.

For a few seconds Ruth lay without moving, so that Simrock began to worry lest she hadn't understood him and he would have to repeat his words. Then at last she opened her eyes, as if after a pause for concentration, and said lightly: "Well, you never know."

She rolled back into her own bed, and Simrock was relieved, and a bit wistful. Sleep gradually returned, and Ruth no longer bothered him with noises. She turned the pages of her novel almost without a sound, only once chuckling softly to herself. Simrock had the feeling that her chuckle was quite unrelated to her book, although it was not unusual for her to laugh while she was reading. He was inclined to think that the chuckle had something to do with him, with something he had said or a look on his face: their ideas of what was funny often differed. He wanted to ask her why she had laughed but realized that he was no longer sufficiently awake to speak.

In the middle of the night he awoke and soon realized that he was not going to be able to fall asleep again. Ruth was breathing without a sound, he had to listen for some time before he could be sure she was lying beside him. Instinct told him it couldn't be later than four. His hand groped across the cool surface of the bedside table and in doing so knocked over his watch. He was too lazy to pick it up right away. The light sound penetrated Ruth's sleep, and she sighed once or twice and shifted her pillow before settling down again. Simrock thought: Ah yes, my heart.

He was relieved to realize that scarcely anything remained of the anxiety that had filled him after the incident at school and that had governed his' thinking up to this moment. Even he now described the episode in his chest as a "so-called" attack, and he attributed his reaction to it to his hitherto unqualified good health, to lack of experience with any deviation from it. A good thing, he thought, that at least Ruth had kept her head, although he still felt that she could have been more sympathetic. He wondered whether any different behavior on Ruth's part might have helped to reassure him, whether perhaps behind her harshness there had after all been genuine concern.

When Ruth's hand happened to fall on his arm and remained there, Simrock made a determined effort to clarify his own wishes. Desire for Ruth was the only unequivocal result, but he found it impossible to wake her and put his arms around her, although he wouldn't have minded much if she had rejected him. He couldn't remember the last time that the desire to make love had become so pent up that even in the middle of the night it obliterated respect for his partner's sleep. Quite apart from the way Ruth might react tonight, he felt that any such behavior would not be appropriate. It was bound to appear contrived, like an uncontrolled outburst of emotions, lip service only.

It felt like a deliverance when the light began imperceptibly to increase and cars started moving. While doing nothing to disturb Ruth's sleep, he hoped that a disturbance from outside would come to his aid. He was almost saved by a truck with a rattling load, but a long time passed before Ruth finally turned her face toward him and said: "Oh, you're awake!"

Simrock nodded in relief.

She asked: "D'you know how you're looking at me?"

Simrock: "How?"

Ruth: "I like it when you look at me like that."

She drew him toward her, while Simrock suddenly thought: It's all wrong, somehow there's something very wrong. But he offered no resistance, he closed his eyes and registered each of her caresses as if he would later have to account for it. He thought: If she hadn't, I would have, one of us had to.

Months later, during what was the mildest winter in years, Simrock stood at the window, looking down into the school playground. He had a free period and was passing the time watching the birds, among which he recognized only the sparrows as sparrows—the crows might be rooks.

He was startled by a hand on his sleeve, having heard no footsteps approaching. The vice principal of the school, Kabitzke, drew him along to his office. He led Simrock like a prisoner through the empty corridor, with exaggerated solemnity, as if he derived pleasure from leaving Simrock in uncertainty for a few moments.

When they were seated facing each other, Kabitzke poured some jasmine tea into two cups. Under Simrock's questioning looks he allowed a long pause to ensue, like someone who, after a forceful but unconsidered beginning, is at a loss how to continue. Simrock would have been glad to help him but hadn't the faintest idea why he had been made to sit down on this uncomfortable chair. With a grin he said: "If it's not convenient today, I can come back another time." Kabitzke, realizing that this wouldn't do, took a deep breath and asked whether Simrock might be feeling the need to unburden himself.

In astonishment Simrock asked: "What gave you that idea, and what do you think is bothering me?"

Kabitzke said: "I hesitate because you might think I am interfering in something that's none of my business."

He broke off again and sipped his tea as if it were boiling hot; Simrock touched his own cup to confirm that the tea was actually lukewarm. Kabitzke's next words sounded as if he were finally sure of the tone he should adopt. Would Simrock be kind enough, he said, not to confuse sympathy with meddling? It was just that he knew from his own, not always pleasant, experience that keeping silent was invariably the least effective way of eliminating problems.

Simrock, now provoked by impatience, said: "I think you've waited long enough to disclose what problems I am suffering from."

Kabitzke now looked him firmly in the eye, as if he knew all about it. Assuming a superior and at the same time wistful expression, he said: "You know, Karl, if we hadn't known each other for ten years, you might have put one over on me. Please don't even try. However, if you believe that I am motivated only by curiosity, then come right out with it, and the matter is closed."

Simrock slapped the palm of his hand on the desk, a little too violently, as he realized in the very act. Forced by his gesture to raise his voice quite a bit, he cried: "For God's sake, tell me what's on your mind! I detest conversations in which one person is kept in the dark by the other."

Kabitzke was not hurt; on the contrary, he seemed to sympathize with Simrock's agitation, with a man in Simrock's position. He placed a hand on his arm, saying it was all right, they would forget all about it; after all, he was quite capable of respecting the reticence of a friend.

Simrock held back his rage, believing that all this wasn't worth having a first quarrel with his vice principal. Moreover, Kabitzke seemed so sincere that he might well be acting with the best of intentions. Simrock thought: But I wish he'd stop patting my arm and acting so soothingly. He yearned for the free period to be over, while Kabitzke poured some more tea and switched the conversation to less mysterious subjects, such as the next union meeting.

After school, Simrock went to a café where he was well known. He went there frequently although not regularly, in fact whenever he didn't feel like facing Ruth right after a day's work and coping with those everyday matters that Ruth would not accept as a woman's business, and in which she was therefore constantly involving him. She worked half days in a state insurance company and so was always home before Simrock; sometimes he was surprised at the long hours he worked.

Simrock was not looking for entertainment at the café, or for distraction; all he did there was exactly what he would have done at home: he prepared his lessons, corrected exercises, or read. The slight bustle didn't bother him, since he did not feel it to be directed at himself, in contrast to lack of quiet at home, against which the only defense was to raise one's voice.

On this particular day, Simrock left exercises and textbooks in his briefcase. He had taken his usual place in the café merely to avoid the effort of having to do something else. He was surprised to see that what he wanted to drink was on the little table before him, coffee and a glass of brandy, although until a moment ago he had been under the impression that the waitress hadn't yet taken his order. He thought: If things have been tolerable so far, why should they suddenly become intolerable?

The brandy tasted worse than usual, it made Simrock

shudder. Nevertheless he ordered another glass, then thought: One thing at a time. If I really want to know what he's been noticing about me, I need only ask him seriously tomorrow. I can't imagine him carrying on indefinitely being so childishly coy and silent. The only question is: Do I care? If he tells me what changes he claims to have noticed in me, that merely concerns my image. But all that matters is whether I have in fact changed and, if so, how. And since when and as a result of what. The second glass of brandy tasted no better than the first, although this time it did not make Simrock shudder.

An elderly lady asked him whether there was room at his table, and with a gesture Simrock offered her the remaining three chairs. He thought: That old fool is right, of course, something has happened. I'm just too lethargic to think it through, and this lethargy is probably at the root of my unhappiness.

The lady asked him the time; Simrock held his wrist-watch up to her eyes. In a flash he saw, clearly and sharply, how carefully he had in the past chased away all the thoughts that had meaning for his existence. As if he had resigned himself to living in an age of extreme division of labor: fundamental things, of whatever kind, were to be the concern of specialists only. In that way amateurs like himself were spared the unspeakable effort of trying to reach the same conclusions, which were not arbitrary but followed the complicated laws of reality. His job, on the other hand, was to devote himself to trifles, of which there were in any case so many that there was precious little time left for anything else. The lady said: "Thank you, I have finished looking at the time."

Simrock apologized and lowered his hand. He said to himself: To continue.

The uneasiness he had been pushing aside, the symptoms of which Kabitzke must have noticed, had started months ago, soon after that slight and as yet nonrecurring pain. It was not the uneasiness that usually precedes important changes; on the contrary, it arose from the certainty that no important changes were to be expected. Although his fear of having heart trouble had evaporated with gratifying speed, a side effect had gained significance: for the first time Simrock was reminded that his life would not last forever, that the time between now and his death at some unspecified point—so the pressure in his chest told him—was nothing but a remainder, large or small, in any case one that was in the process of diminishing. He tried to face with derision the disagreeable shudder that followed, reminding himself that anyone who confused truisms with insights had good reason to suffer from his error. If I am depressed by the thought that, the longer I live, the closer my death approaches, I should also be disturbed by the fact that series do exist, that things don't all happen side by side, simultaneously and perpetually. Or he told himself that anyone who suffers from the inevitable, from the inexorable, is bound to end up in a neurosis.

But the peace of mind that he acquired by means of these speculations appeared suspect to him from the very outset, like a suit whose seams held only for as long as the wearer didn't move.

The lady asked him for a light, he offered it, and took care to flick the lighter shut and lower his hand as soon as the cigarette was lit. The lady thanked him in a tone of voice indicating that a conversation could now be regarded as under way. Simrock pushed the ashtray toward her. I've been kidding myself, he thought, to try to persuade myself that I'm suffering from something inevitable, inexorable: actually, what's tormenting me is not that the number of years remaining to me is constantly diminishing, but that, unless something decisive occurs, I shall be spending those years in such a meaningless way. Although I've never admitted it to myself, I have led my whole life so far as if the genuinely important things were still to come. I have been waiting for the door to be opened behind which the action is taking place. I never asked myself whose hand was supposed to turn the doorknob. Surely it's normal for a fifteen-year-old to pin his greatest hopes on the future. I wouldn't even know how to answer if someone were to ask me what my hopes were.

Then he thought: All major decisions that it was up to me to make were made long ago. My marriage is an accomplished fact, my profession laid down. When I look at my marriage and my teaching career, I have the feeling that both follow rules established without my having been consulted; nevertheless, it all began with my own decision. In the years that followed, no further decisions faced me. The responsibilities were allotted, and I approved. At least until this hour, I never raised any objections. If I should ever decide to challenge the rules—and at the moment I feel the urge to do so—I must reckon with meeting resistance. Those whose authority I would like to challenge will call me a mischiefmaker.

When Simrock's eyes chanced to meet those of the elderly lady, she asked: "I suppose you're thinking about very serious matters?" Simrock replied: "I am thinking about how I could radically change my life. However, I haven't reached complete clarity yet."

The lady gave Simrock a long look. She hesitated to show an interest, being no longer sure whether someone who had reacted so unaccountably to a kindly question was a suitable partner for an afternoon's chat. She glanced at the empty brandy glass, then back at Simrock, who had decided that he had done enough thinking for the day. Important decisions, however urgent, should not, he felt, be made in haste.

The first thing to do, Simrock told himself, in order not to be at the mercy of future events like a leaf in the wind, was to draft a kind of plan for the new start:

Since habits ease the human situation, whereas the person making a new start wishes to break with habits, tensions are unavoidable. So as a first step Simrock decided not to be taken unawares by tensions but to await them calmly. Then: Not to be ashamed of revising attitudes, of becoming a different person in the eyes of others. Since it was this very dissatisfaction with the person one had been yesterday that set the change in motion, being ashamed would merely indicate halfheartedness. The best thing to do: hold one's new attitude aloft like a banner high over one's head, to flaunt it until one gradually takes it for granted.

Then: To examine what one has deemed necessary. Examine possessions deemed necessary, discover how much ballast they conceal; the same thing with modes of behavior deemed necessary. Scrutinize wishes deemed necessary. How many of those could one discard without reducing one's expectations for the future? Even a single discarded wish can have its consequences. To abandon wishes means to release capacity. Next comes a phase of utmost concentration: to bring the unacknowledged wishes to the surface. That won't happen at once, it's not a matter of minutes. To keep on asking oneself whether the unacknowledged wishes are not the truly important ones. And when one finally recognizes these wishes, or suspects their existence—not to be alarmed by them. To be careful in branding something as *deviant, deviant* being a favorite expression of the opponents of change.

To make a clear distinction between scruple and cowardice, so as to avoid confusion. To scrutinize whether one isn't also confusing something else—on the one hand, wanting to have certain wishes; on the other hand, wishing. But not to spend too much time on scrutiny, scrutiny can become an excuse. To accept the wishes thus recognized, to acknowledge them, at first only to oneself.

To accept the fact that a period of disagreement is beginning; more specifically, of open nonagreement. A period of battles minor or major, depending; it won't be entirely up to you. While striving to eliminate this nonagreement, to remain aware that a state of disunity is a permanent one and there is nothing intrinsically shameful about it. A fleeting dream of happiness: being accepted in spite of nonagreement, being allowed to persist in nonagreement without risking the withdrawal of love. To have the feeling that disagreeing is not merely tolerated but essential, that it is needed and expected in order that its causes may not be overlooked. Love could be like that.

Then: To breathe life into the generally accepted claim that every development is marked by contradictions. To apply this to oneself. To reverse it at some point: to what extent are the contradictions marked by a development?

To continue: How does one learn to advance to one's outer limits? Essential to examine whether some cunning system of miscalculation, fear, lethargy, and self-deception is not blocking access to these limits. Like a wall inside the country, far from the actual frontier. To regard the thrust to this frontier as important, the most important thing of all. Not to be deterred by the usual reproach that one is motivated by self-love and selfishness.

Rather, to believe that it is only in these outer limits that the power to be of use mysteriously grows; that only there is one able to abandon the role of minion, which entails, in addition to its disadvantages, the advantage of a humdrum security. Hence to participate in some public activity in which, in moments of honesty, one doubted whether one had ever really participated. Because one couldn't imagine how. By saying nothing?

To sum up: To endeavor finally to live according to the most recent level of one's insights. And to endeavor to be sincere. Not just at times when sincerity is permitted, but always. Or almost always, or as often as possible. As often as one's strength allows. And then: Not to make a principle of disagreeing, not a rule, or to make agreeing the exception. Not to fall from the extreme of invariably agreeing into the extreme of invariably rejecting. In every instance to make a fresh decision, to keep on deciding, never again to stop deciding.

And to trust one's conviction, but not to take it for granted. To be on the lookout for better and better justification for it. To be able to say: On that subject I have no opinion. To be concerned that in earlier times such words would never have been uttered. To ask oneself: Why not? To discover one's opinions, finally to discover one's opinions in that great heap of opinions, in order calmly to identify oneself. These were the things that Simrock mulled over during the following weeks.

For weeks he searched for a beginning. Some evenings he got drunk, sometimes so drunk that Leonie was scared and complained to her mother. When he was sober again, Ruth would admonish him at least to show some consideration for the child. Simrock then became particularly affectionate toward Leonie. He could explain nothing to Ruth; he couldn't tell her that he got drunk in cold blood, so to speak, not to gratify an urge but in the hope that alcohol would show him a way that he couldn't find when he was sober.

However, he soon abandoned this method on noting that he had miscalculated and was an obnoxious drunk who in no way resembled the image of a drunk he had when he was sober. Ruth was overjoyed at this transformation; she kissed Simrock on his second sober evening and was exuberant at the supper table. To Leonie she said: "Dad has come to his senses again, thank God."

It was gradually borne in on Simrock that it wasn't enough merely to try to account for his disgust but that, in order to get going, he would have to find out more about his desires. To cease to want something, he told himself, was not an adequate program. He found this train of thought conclusive, relaxed somewhat in it, and felt that, if he concentrated long enough on it, a passable route into the future must, in the long run, materialize. Then he believed he had discovered what his first step must be: to leave Ruth. This conviction was so compelling that he wondered where his wits had been all this time. For several minutes his only thought was: But of course! Then: If a person is sure of a thing, he needn't spend much time looking for arguments.

He made Ruth sit down facing him. His solemn demeanor caused her to look at him expectantly, but he could not bring himself to divulge his plan. Instead, he stroked her hand and decided to wait for a more favorable opportunity, for the next quarrel perhaps. He was determined not to pick a quarrel, although that would have required little effort. At all costs it must be a credible quarrel, evolving logically and inevitably; a deliberately provoked quarrel would seem deceitful to him. But at the same time he told himself that excessive compassion would prevent him from carrying out a task he knew to be unavoidable; as it was, it would prove difficult enough.

For a week Simrock was more considerate than he had been for a long time. He avoided every thoughtless word. There were moments when he even enjoyed the calm that seemed never-ending and forgot what he was so impatiently waiting for. Then again the calm would oppress him, and he would wonder how long he could put up with it.

This indecisive state lasted until Ruth said he seemed like a different person. Simrock reacted sharply. There being nothing at which he could direct his rage, he said in a loud and exasperated voice: "I'd like to know what I have done to deserve your mockery. If this one peaceful week is more than you can stand, just let me know."

Ruth asked what in the world made him feel mocked, to which Simrock replied: "For days I have been making a supreme effort, which has obviously not escaped your notice, to take the tension out of our relationship. It is now quite clear to me that all you do is calmly look on, that you have folded your arms and are observing my efforts as if they didn't concern you."

Ruth said: "That sounds like someone who is spoiling for a fight."

Simrock felt she had seen through him; now the very thing had happened that he had wanted at all costs to avoid. He put his arms around her, not only to escape her line of vision but also because he felt they could both use a little tenderness at the moment. Ruth seemed to be holding back during his embrace, to be covertly observing his every movement as if not trusting his change of mood. Simrock released her, and they went into their friendly room.

He awoke later from a dream that had left him with an unpleasant memory, though he had forgotten what it was about. He thought: I have decided on a course, and I know my intentions to be good and proper. But whenever I am about to open my mouth, I feel I'm putting myself in the wrong. Circumstances are against me.

He got up and went into the kitchen, where he sat down at the table; it was not long before he started to weep. That surprised him, and he went over to the mirror and looked in amazement at the weeping face. He had not noticed the approach of tears: suddenly they were there. He washed his face, found a piece of paper, and sat down again. He wrote: *How can I contrive a situation in which it is possible to discuss the unavoidable changes with Ruth?*

He stared at this sentence for a long time, until he felt an urge to crumple up the paper and with it all thoughts of the recent past. It was a desire to let himself fall, sink back in indifference; but a disgust—which he did not feel at the moment but which he knew would certainly return—warned him. How, he thought, can I contrive it?

He recalled an incident of many years before: The wife of one of his friends is suddenly taken ill, whereupon this friend gives Simrock two tickets for an opening. Simrock is sitting with Ruth at the movie. Before it starts, while the lights are still on, Ruth asks whether he doesn't agree that there is a funny kind of atmosphere in the theater. He doesn't know what she means, tells her reassuringly that she isn't used to the atmosphere of movie premieres, that this is what premieres are like. Ruth says No, she is sure it is something else, but she can't express it more clearly. Simrock also recalled his words: "You with your second sight." The film starts, and in watching it they forget Ruth's premonition. The screening seems to be proceeding normally until, about halfway through, an indignant male voice calls out, asking how long the audience is expected to put up with this. Ruth seizes Simrock's hand and whispers: "What did I tell you!" Simrock also remembered his sudden fear, for no one as yet had ever called out in a movie theater while he was there. And Ruth had had a premonition. Another man shouts that the first heckler should shut his paid mouth and go home, no one was forcing him to stay. Some members of the audience actually do leave, some whistle or scrape their feet, catcalls persist till the end of the performance. Simrock would like to leave, too, but is held back by curiosity. He whispers: "Shall we leave?" Ruth nervously shakes her head. Simrock is no longer looking at the screen, what he wants to see now is real life. He would like to see a heckler, he would like to see an outraged face. For his impression is that the outrage is false, brought into the theater rather than originating here, an outrage evenly distributed among the rows of seats. The scripts of these people seem uninspired. Someone shouts: "This is an insult to our Party!" Someone shouts: "Boo! Stop the show! Boo! Turn on the lights!" After the performance, groups of people stand about in the street arguing, and Simrock draws Ruth toward the spot where there seems to be the greatest commotion. The violent words he hears hardly differ from those that were shouted in the movie theater. Simrock wonders why two men so obviously of the same opinion are conversing in such loud voices. Shortly afterward, the movie is banned; there is no mention of it in the newspapers. It met with outraged rejection on the part of the public, a docent explains to the teachers at a meeting, and Simrock can't pluck up enough courage to call him a liar.

He decided simply to tell Ruth outright. Anything else, he felt as he sat at the kitchen table, would seem like setting a trap for her. To wait for a quarrel, he told himself that night, was in fact tantamount to provoking it, and in a particularly cold-blooded and dishonorable way. Moreover, he doubted whether he had sufficient histrionic talents to declare his decision during some future quarrel in such a way that it would sound spontaneous. How wretched Ruth would feel were she to see through the ploy! If, on the other hand, he were to declare his decision at some random time, for no other reason than that he intended to live without Ruth, then there was nothing to see through. The new era, he told himself, must not begin with subterfuge.

Simrock turned out the light, went to the window, and looked down into the black street. Nothing was moving, only a neon sign flickered some distance away, in the building across the street one window showed a light. After concentrating long enough, he thought he could make out a woman. He fetched his binoculars; it was an elderly woman sitting at a table in her pajamas, reading a book. The glasses were not powerful enough to give a clear view of her face, but, from the eagerness with which she turned a page, Simrock gathered that whatever she was reading kept her in suspense. He stood at the window until something did move, a police car drove leisurely along the street.

The next day he took Ruth's hand, saying: "I'd like us to separate. I have waited a long time for an opportunity that would make it easier for us, but I never found one. On some days my reasons seem to me convincing, on others they don't. The most important reason is: if we were to meet for the first time today, the way we are now, it wouldn't occur to either of us to marry the other. There is hardly anything left of either of us with which the other could fall in love. Since I know perfectly well that it wasn't always like that, I ask myself what it is that has changed us so."

Only now did Simrock become aware of the contrast between his words and his gesture—he was still holding Ruth's hand. He let go of it. Ruth looked at him coldly, unapproachably. Simrock knew that her face almost automatically took on this expression as soon as she heard something that upset her. He said: "I remember how years ago we used to point out each other's mistakes, our flaws. That had nothing to do with picking quarrels; though sometimes it may have looked like that to an outsider, we knew better. It was just as important to us for the other to be always in the right as to be in the right ourselves. To leave the other knowingly in the wrong would have seemed like betrayal. The word for this is empathy. Today we are concerned with each other's mistakes only when those mistakes annoy us. And along with our loss of interest in each other's mistakes is our loss of interest in each other's good qualities. Because our lovable qualities are no longer in demand, they are atrophying."

Simrock smoked as he waited tensely for a reply, thinking: It's entirely up to her whether we part on good terms or bad. But Ruth said nothing, wasn't even looking at him now, as if politeness alone were keeping her on her chair. Simrock said: "I feel you should know that I have often spent half the day wandering around town just to avoid being at home. And I don't even like being in town, it's crowded and noisy and uncomfortable. But I stay on, in no hurry to come home, and thinking: Perhaps something will turn up. I keep telling myself that the chances of anything turning up are very remote. But our marriage gives me no hope at all. The worst thing I can blame you for is that I can't stand myself any more. To suspect that probably the reverse is true doesn't help me one bit. Nor am I prepared to go on regarding our friendly room as a solution. Sometimes a disaster plan is set up at a time when disaster seems out of the question. That's exactly what's happened to us with our absurd bedroom rules. We can only lie together because we disown each other, and because we disown each other we commit rape on each other. The fact that this rape occurs by mutual consent doesn't make it any less offensive."

As he spoke, Simrock wondered how Ruth was reacting. He was by no means sure whether what seemed so convincing to him was equally convincing to her. What would be her reasons, he asked himself, for withholding her consent to a separation? Fear of material consequences seemed unlikely, since Ruth had an agreeably casual attitude toward property; besides, he was prepared to make any concessions. With even greater certainty, he excluded the possibility of love as a stumbling block. What he did think possible was fear of the unknown situation, fear of the very thing he longed for.

He said: "We can't burden our child with a continuation of our marriage, either. She's suffering from the chilly atmosphere. She's excluded from our few moments of illusory warmth. This is not to say that I want to leave you for Leonie's sake—I am acting entirely selfishly. But I would like you to think of that aspect, too, before you give me your answer. I have been noticing for quite some time that Leonie is becoming more and more withdrawn, that we are gradually forfeiting the chance to influence her, except by force. Her parents are her only example, so it seems natural to her to be withdrawn."

Ruth continued to sit there as if she were not interested. She allowed the pauses Simrock made to pass unused, nor did it look as if she could bring herself to comment even if these pauses were any longer. Simrock's gaze roamed over her body, and he saw that she wasn't moving a finger or rocking a foot. She didn't even ask for a cigarette, which normally at the slightest upset she couldn't do without. Simrock thought: She's sitting so still because she's watching herself and doesn't know how to react. Pity rose in him, and he had to keep himself from taking her hand again.

Instead, he held out his lighted cigarette, and Ruth finished it, inhaling deeply. Simrock felt relieved, because her accepting the cigarette seemed to indicate that Ruth was now ready to talk.

He thought it possible that the only thing holding her back might be the very first word, so he asked: "Won't you tell me how you feel about all this?"

Ruth said: "That's really quite irrelevant. When all's said and done, it's the one holding the pistol who always gets his way."

He asked: "What pistol?"

Stretching out his hands, he turned the palms up and then down again, but even before replacing his hands on his knees he found his movements ridiculous. Ruth appeared to overlook the foolishness and to be pondering how she could best make herself understood. Then she struck him in the face with full force. Simrock felt a burning pain as a fingernail tore a bit of skin from his nose. He leaped up in a fit of rage and grabbed her wrists. Ruth looked him coolly in the eye as if curious to see what he would do next.

It took a few seconds for him to regain control of himself in his pain. He thought: Of course I won't touch her. It was crazy to behave as if we could discuss splitting up like the weather. It's probably a good thing she hit me. I must keep alive the memory of the pain and the hatred in her eyes, I can always fall back on that.

Ruth said: "You're hurting me."

Simrock let go of her wrists, which looked alarmingly white. Ruth massaged them while Simrock dabbed at a drop of blood on his nose with a handkerchief. They turned away from each other, as people do when they don't want their actions to be observed.

After some time Ruth said: "You know, I can explain your decision. It's because you are so unhappy about their having broken your back at school that you want to leave us. You're thinking of separation as a first step, and at the same time you're scared stiff that you'll never take the second. This fear is now strengthening your resolve. I am telling you this, not to persuade you to come back, for I would imagine that marriage with a man who has to be persuaded to stay is even more hellish than ours has been. I am only telling you in order that this important factor may not escape you. Accept it as a farewell gift, maybe you can find a use for it."

Feeling that her words would acquire too much weight if he let them pass unchallenged, Simrock wanted to make some reply. Ruth stood for a few seconds as though waiting for just that. But everything that passed through his mind seemed insignificant, not worth the bother of forming into sentences. Ruth left the room. Simrock wondered whether her ability to appear composed in even the most unpleasant situations had been more of a help or a hindrance to their life together over the years. He was inclined toward the negative view since, under the circumstances, he had to regard his marriage as being on the rocks. Never having been in the position of needing to console her, he suddenly felt an urge to console someone. It struck him that he had never once seen Ruth cry. Perhaps, he thought, her striking him had been a sort of crying.

Ruth said she had neither intended nor instigated the separation and was therefore not prepared to exchange their apartment for two smaller ones. If Simrock felt such an irresistible urge for an upheaval, she said scornfully, he would have to accept the discomforts involved, such as having to look for new accommodation, whether he liked it or not. Or did he actually expect Leonie and her to pay half of a price that would never have been necessary if he hadn't gone off his rocker? Simrock inferred from her words an awkwardly formulated, final attempt at reconciliation.

"No," he said, "I don't expect that, and we needn't waste words about it. We must try to behave now in such a way that we retain pleasant memories of each other."

Ruth said: "I couldn't care less what kind of an image you retain of me."

There was no escape for Simrock from the odious procedure of having to go to the housing authorities, be placed on a waiting list, and wait several years for an apartment. But since he had no intention of sitting out those years in their shared apartment—which, incidentally, Ruth would have had no power to prevent—he had to look around for a stopgap. The possibilities were limited, since most of Simrock's friends lived in apartments which it would have meant considerable sacrifice to share with him. And in cases where space might have allowed this, he was ashamed to make known his needs. Nor was it fear of refusal that prevented him, for he would have fully understood if some of them had been unwilling to forfeit so much freedom of movement. Simrock's embarrassment arose from a different quandary: he did not feel close enough to any of these eligible apartment dwellers to be justified in asking for the loan of a room. He knew from experience how easily those in need transgress the limits of modesty in their requests and become a nuisance.

Simrock recalled the father of one of his students, who had approached him some time before with the request that his son be given a better mark in social sciences on his report card than the failing one Simrock had intimated. When Simrock asked what possible reason there was for him to make such a change, the father replied that his brother, the boy's uncle, and he, Simrock, had been classmates. Simrock had first assumed that this was by way of introducing some further explanation to incline him toward leniency. But when it dawned on him that this was the sum total of the father's arguments, he replied that he was genuinely sorry but he had made it a principle to cheat only in behalf of members of the immediate family. Thus if the father himself had been his classmate, he said with a straight face, the matter could have been discussed. But since it had been only the boy's uncle, and moreover, as he well remembered, a thoroughly obnoxious fellow, he could not see his way clear to doing anything about the failing mark. Simrock warned himself: Under no circumstances take a room with people who might be too diffident to cope with the importunities of a sponger.

On the other hand, he reflected, integrity and tact required the presence of certain resources to fall back on, and he had enough imagination to predict how fast his reserve of both would dwindle if he were to continue to live under one roof with Ruth for any length of time. Alternatively, he foresaw that his plans would be buried under the daily grind, and of this he was equally afraid.

One after another he called upon three people he knew and made his request. Rather than select those whose accommodation was largest in relation to the number of occupants, he picked those with whom he could adopt a casual tone. The negative result matched his expectations. The first, over tea and cookies, made such strenuous efforts to direct the conversation to some other topic that Simrock could not bring himself to repeat his request. The second man, a former colleague who was now a coach at an athletic club, placed his arm sympathetically around Simrock's shoulders and promised him full support. It went without saying that in an emergency—by which he meant: with a girl—Simrock could spend the night at his place, there was absolutely no question. Simrock, by this time more determined than on his first attempt, made a great effort to clear up the misunderstanding; but the former colleague persisted stubbornly, until Simrock got the message and capitulated.

His highest hopes were for the last attempt. This third acquaintance was himself divorced and had retained possession of the apartment, his wife having left him for a foreigner in the diplomatic service. Simrock did not particularly care for him. They had known each other at the university, Simrock considered him ruthless and dissolute, and at first this opinion had made him hesitate to place the third name on his short list. What finally tipped the scales was the thought that the very dissoluteness of the fellow offered some prospect of success. Simrock was received in high good humor and at first couldn't get in a single word, he was led from room to room and obliged to admire some new furniture. He noticed that the man had had a few drinks, although there was no evidence of bottle or glass. Simrock wondered, while the other man never stopped talking, whether it wasn't immoral to come out at this particular moment with a question that required an absolutely clear head for an answer. Then he told himself: To ask my question of a drunk is not nearly so reprehensible as I shall be unhappy if I don't find a room soon. Finally he took advantage of a pause and told the fellow the reason for his visit. The latter was silent for a few moments, as if finding it difficult to grasp what Simrock actually expected of him. Then, after a little smile, he took three hundred marks from a drawer and placed them on the table. Simrock now remembered that this was a man who had owed him money for so long that he had written it off years ago and later forgotten all about it. Instantly he grasped the connection between his question and the repayment of the money: since the man could not count on the forgetfulness of his creditor, he did not want the old debt to stand in the way of refusing Simrock's proposal. Simrock would not have credited him with so much sensitivity. He pocketed the money and shortly afterward listened to a straight refusal of his request, unmitigated by any excuse. When he left he felt relieved.

A goddamned room to himself, he swore under his breath. He began to wonder whether an obstacle of this kind might be enough to block his future. Ruth said: "Why don't you move in with your mother for the time being?" Simrock replied by saying something that until then he had only dared to think: "I can't stand her."

As far back as he could remember, he had scarcely a single pleasant memory of his mother, apart from those that had to do with satisfying his needs. How vivid, on the other hand, were the memories of yelling and coldness, of arguments over his neglect of useless tasks, conducted so grimly that the consequences invariably triggered the next quarrel. Simrock now suspected that his mother had never forgiven him for the fact that the day of his birth had put an end to her girlhood. When he was sixteen she had confided to him, as if it were a deep, dark secret, that she and his father had got married only five months before he was born. Five months, she had said, you know what that means! Their marriage had been in a permanent state of strife. His mother had played the role of the wife who sacrifices too much—that is, herself—for her little family and who has the experience day after day of seeing that no one appreciates her selflessness. After his father's death Simrock had visited her regularly—as a son with a sense of duty—but rarely at intervals of less than a month. At first it had required a particular effort to make these visits, convinced as he was that his mother had no small share in his father's death. The doctor had diagnosed heart failure, but Simrock had told her: "If no one had persuaded him that he was good for nothing and uncouth and in fact merely tolerated, he might in his clumsy way be alive today." When he gradually found it possible to establish a calm relationship with his mother, the tension between them relaxed. Sometimes he defended her in his own eyes by accusing himself of having always seen her as a finished person and never as a creature with a history that he had never tried to explore. During his visits they usually discussed uncontroversial topics. He would fix light switches or dripping faucets, and his mother seemed to like having a son who could be handy around the house.

Ruth had reminded Simrock of a possibility he had already considered himself and rejected, for to ask his mother for a room seemed humiliating. He knew he could not count on Ruth's sympathy; that was understandable, and he sighed.

As he entered the hall, he was met by the smell of a cheap cigar. His mother, whose self-assurance he always envied, seemed embarrassed when she told him she had a visitor in the living room. Simrock drew her into the kitchen. He had made up his mind to discuss his problems about finding a room as briefly as possible, fearing that ten minutes' conversation with her might deprive him of the necessary inclination or courage. He had even come prepared with some phrases.

His mother listened to his concise report, in which he explained nothing, in which he merely outlined the circumstances and the resultant dilemma. Without putting it into so many words, Simrock made it quite clear that he had come not to consult her but only to find out whether she could let him have the little room at the end of the hall for a limited time. Without hesitation his mother said: "Of course you can stay here."

For a few seconds they looked at each other seriously; each time Simrock saw her she seemed smaller and slighter. Her face, he felt, expressed more curiosity than sympathy. She patted his knee a few times, as if he needed encouraging. Simrock reflected that she had never liked Ruth, that the cordiality she had shown her had seemed insincere from the very first day, and that Leonie, unlike other children with their grandmothers, had made a point of avoiding her. His mother got up and asked him to wait a moment.

She left the room, and Simrock thought: Like it or not, I should be pleased at the result. He would start moving this very day. Ruth's eyes, he thought, when I take my underwear out of the drawer and put it in my suitcase. Even in the kitchen, he now noticed, the smell of that cigar still hung in the air. Curious, Simrock opened the door, first a crack, and then, finding the hall empty, wide. Of the conversation taking place in the living room he could not distinguish a single word. Hanging on the clothes stand was an overcoat—too heavy for the mild April weather—and beside it a double-breasted jacket with a white handkerchief stuck in the outside breast pocket. Simrock said: "Lady's man!" On the floor, next to his mother's shoes, he saw a pair of men's shoes, black and so shiny as to be laughable. He knocked on the living-room door. Sitting in the only armchair was a man wearing horizontally striped suspenders who stared with hostility at Simrock and ignored his courteous greeting. Simrock found him much too old, much too decrepit, for his attractive mother. He asked her how soon he could bring over his things.

His mother said: "Today, if you like."

The man stood up, and Simrock was surprised to see how

tall he was. He walked past Simrock out of the room, leaving the door open. His mother made appeasing gestures, which Simrock did not understand. The man returned carrying a Swissair holdall. Picking up a cardigan from the sofa, he began carefully folding it. Simrock would have liked to make himself scarce yet wondered whether his mother might not be glad of his presence. The man, while holding the neck of the cardigan tucked under his chin, said pleadingly: "Couldn't we possibly . . ."

Simrock's mother replied, quickly and decisively: "No, we most certainly could not."

Her retort sounded scathing, and Simrock could guess what lay behind it. Evidently she was just as highhanded with this man as she had been with his father. In a whisper his mother told him she was quite capable of coping with the situation on her own, and Simrock marveled at her perspicacity. He said he would be back the following afternoon with his suitcases, but as it turned out he arrived five days late.

The first few evenings he went for long walks, not merely to get acquainted with the new district. He felt the urge to be alone, and once he thought: Good God, if I don't want to be with Leonie and Ruth, then I certainly don't want to be with other people—as if he owed Ruth and Leonie an interim period of solitude. The last thing he wanted was to sit around with his mother and be quizzed as to why his marriage had broken up. Even so, he found, he was with her more than enough; she insisted on making his breakfast every morning, on sitting with him while he ate it, and, when she was not plying him with questions, on talking away until he closed the front door behind him. There was no escape from hundreds of details of her life. On one occasion, while walking along a dark avenue, he wished he could take an interest in all these details. He had to listen to the origin and course of his mother's relationship with Richard, the man with the shiny shoes, and how it had finally reached a stage that, even without Simrock's turning up, would have made its rupture inevitable. Simrock regarded these morning chronicles as a kind of rent, a condition for the use of the room at the end of the hall. It was on walks, he believed, that he could do his best thinking, and even a light rain did not bother him. But sometimes, after returning home, he found he had forgotten which thoughts had occupied him on the walk. The walks induced in him a trancelike state in which the past dissolved, the future lost all significance, and his worries became weightless. Then later, as he mounted the stairs in his mother's building and became aware of the present, he reproached himself with having frittered away another evening. How in the world, he wondered once, did I get into this mess?

Once he wandered aimlessly through his childhood. The house stands in a sun-filled street, set back from the sidewalk by a bed of tired flowers. He dare not tell his mother how bored he is, for she always finds chores for him. The flower bed must be watered each evening, even in winter it must never be stepped on. It is surrounded by an iron railing, six inches above the ground, as wide as a man's thumb. Albrecht from next door can walk along this railing as easily as on the ground, ten times back and forth if he likes. He, Simrock, can never do it, either fast or slow; a few times he gets almost to the middle. As he steps onto the railing he knows he won't make it, even before he steps onto it. Maybe that's where his mistake lies. Maybe it would be easier if one were to tell oneself that there is nothing to walking on the railing. He tells himself this for half a day, but then after only three steps he can't stay up there. He practices until his mother sees him through the window and has a chore for him. The name of the little town is Prenzlau. Albrecht finds the railing a bore, he says: Once you've done it you can always do it! Karl cries in bed.

Suddenly Simrock found himself surrounded by a silent gang of youths. He hadn't seen them even a second earlier, they must have emerged from a hiding place that might have been any shrub bordering the avenue. The very instant Simrock realized they meant to rob him, he was seized by several hands. The hands did not seem brutal, or particularly strong, but there were so many that it would have been pointless to fight back. The only point, Simrock thought, would have been the satisfaction of fighting back, and he didn't move. He was surprised to find how calmly he was facing the incident, which was unprecedented in his experience, how he felt almost like a spectator who has already seen something similar in a movie. The light from the nearest street lamp, at least twenty yards away, was not enough for him to distinguish faces clearly. Simrock saw only fleeting details emerging from the darkness, frightened eyes, a heavy chain around a wrist, a mouth gaping in excitement. Then he felt rapid fingers searching through his pockets and sliding between his shirt and jacket, and he thought he could tell that they were hardly expert in tracking down loot. When they had found his wallet and change purse and stashed them away in the dark but were still continuing their search, Simrock thought: How many wallets and change purses do they think I carry around? Then he heard a girl's voice calling: "The fuzz!" Instantly the muggers let go of him and scattered in various directions. Simrock snatched at one of the hands, the last one to be withdrawn from his pockets. A fist struck his hip, then he found to his amazement that he had taken a prisoner. The youth tried desperately to free himself, but Simrock was by far the stronger. He twisted the writhing arm to a point where the slightest pressure was enough to cause agonizing pain. The youth kicked out once at Simrock's shin, then yelped and gave up. At this point Simrock saw the policeman. He was approaching on the other side of the road, strolling along on his evening beat. Simrock considered how much precise information he could actually supply. He did not know how many members there were in the gang, he had heard no names, and there was not one face he would have recognized in its entirety. He did not even know how much money there had been in his wallet. Then he thought: What nonsense, I am holding the most precise information right here by the hand. But then, when the policeman was level with them, he could not bring himself to call out. He saw the beads of sweat on the boy's forehead and the hatred in his eyes, which were looking not at the policeman, but straight at him. The policeman paid no attention to them, perhaps he was not even aware of them. A movie scene, Simrock thought again. For a moment he was about to let go of the boy, then he considered the possibility of getting back his property in exchange. He thought: A hostage. His eyes followed the policeman and he decided to let him walk three street lamps farther before starting a discussion that might become noisy.

He considered which method offered the greatest prospect of success: behaving as a lenient adult, as a stern educator, or as the stronger one who counters violence with violence. Then he realized that the decision had already been made, that violence was already being applied; one point in his favor in the boy's eyes might be that he had let the policeman go by without saying a word. Deep in these thoughts, Simrock was unable to react quickly enough when the boy wrenched himself free. Simrock stood there undecided and annoyed, and before he could take even one step in pursuit there was nothing left of the boy but the direction in which he had taken off into the trees and shrubs. Simrock made a gesture of resignation. He dreaded the explanations to be given, the forms to be filled out, the trips to be made, before his identity card and other papers were replaced. He wanted a victory, any kind of a victory among the many defeats. He continued on his way, now no longer a walk, and told himself it had been stupid to assume that the boy he had caught would feel any sympathy for him because he hadn't involved the police. Rather, it now seemed to him, his decision not to call the policeman must have struck the boy as alarming. Had he been arrested, there would have been, from the boy's point of view, unpleasant but predictable consequences, at any rate roughly according to the rules of the game. The uncertain future, however, behind the backs of the police, in the grip of that ice-cold man, might turn out to be a nightmare—he might have fallen, say, into the hands of a sadist. Simrock reasoned that consequently a benefactor would do well to lose no time acquainting those concerned with his good intentions.

A few yards ahead of him a little package dropped onto the path. Simrock could not locate the thrower anywhere, it must have flown out from the shrubbery. He prodded it cautiously with his foot, something light, wrapped in newspaper. He was sure he was being observed. He picked up the package and in it found his wallet and change purse. The wallet contained all his papers, and Simrock put it in his pocket, along with the change purse, without checking its contents. He was convinced that not a pfennig was missing. Before going on he wondered whether, in the sudden wave of happiness that went through him, he should call out something in the direction of the shrubbery.

Simrock was summoned to Kabitzke. Kabitzke said: "You're getting yourself into trouble for absolutely no reason.

42

Perhaps you've gone out of your mind. Or do you feel you have to attract attention at any price?"

Simrock said: "I would find it easier to answer if I knew what you were driving at."

Kabitzke opened his notebook and studied it with an expression that suggested things were going desperately wrong for Simrock. Simrock saw him as a man who fought his battle against uneventfulness by consistently and prematurely sounding the alarm. When the anticipated disasters failed to materialize, he would attribute this to his having issued a warning in good time. But nobody laughed at him.

Kabitzke said: "Precisely nine of your students turned up at the May Day demonstration."

Simrock: "I know, I was there myself."

Kabitzke: "This inadequate attendance was preceded by an outrageous incident: you told the class that only those who wished to needed to go to the demonstration; those wishing to do something else should feel free to do so. Is that correct or not?"

Simrock: "Yes, that's correct. As far as I know, attending demonstrations is voluntary, and that's what I pointed out."

Kabitzke: "Voluntary, voluntary! Don't give me that!"

Simrock: "Allow me to stress an important point. I did not try to influence the kids to stay away from the demonstration, I wanted to encourage them to make up their own minds. Incidentally, I started with a detailed account of the history of May Day. I really don't know why you are so upset."

Kabitzke: "I'll tell you why. There are people who see your conspicuous emphasis on the voluntary aspect of attendance as an act of defiance."

Simrock: "I'm sorry to hear that. If you wish, I can explain to each of them that all I had in mind was to prevent any of the kids from feeling obliged to join in the demonstration."

Kabitzke: "For Christ's sake, this is no time to play dumb."

Simrock: "I agree. If I interpret your words correctly, I am now under a misapprehension. I shall take the next opportunity of telling the class that attendance in demonstrations is obligatory after all, that each of them has either to appear or to furnish a written excuse. If there are any questions, I shall refer them to you."

Kabitzke: "Like hell you will."

Simrock smiled before saying: "To my mind we have now arrived at an extremely important point. You obviously wish for attendance in certain events to be called voluntary but for me to see to it that all my students turn out in a body. This is asking too much of me, so in future I shall no longer recognize any difference between actual and alleged voluntary attendance."

Kabitzke: "Karl, it's impossible to talk sense with you. I find what you're saying irresponsible, to my ears it sounds self-destructive."

Simrock slapped the desk with the palm of his hand. In the pause that ensued, while Kabitzke looked at him incredulously, he told himself that from his side there was nothing more to add. Then he remembered that not long ago he had slapped the same table, and it occurred to him that Kabitzke must soon regard his desk-slapping as a silly habit. He stood up and left the office. For a few minutes he was pleased to have been the one who had put an end to the conversation.

Since deep within him, as Simrock was ashamed to acknowledge during the next few days, lay the conviction that he could not help his students, he shut himself off from them and acquired the reputation of being a strict teacher. And yet he knew that actually they liked him, for he did his best not to violate his students' sense of fairness. Nor did he demand any senseless discipline; if they forgot some of the prescribed forms of respect, they did not have to worry about being penalized. Simrock's theory was that he and the class formed a kind of working partnership whose effectiveness was only to be measured by how much of what the teacher said stayed put in the students' heads. He avoided familiarity because he imagined it might be a source of favoritism and discrimination; to be equally familiar with all seemed impossible. The students could be sure that inattention or laziness would invariably result in poor marks, and that was why, Simrock assumed, they regarded him as strict.

He told himself: It's no use closing my eyes any longer to the fact that the crucial changes must take place in school. My plans can never be realized so long as I behave as if the tough problems will take care of themselves. So far, he thought, I have broken through the ring around me at its weakest point, my family. I am living in a cave like a fox, I'm lonely, unhappy, going to seed. Is this the sum total of my success? The expectations, he thought, without which my present life would be hell have no justification whatever if I sit here twiddling my thumbs.

Simrock proceeded to explore which of the attributes of the teacher he had been up to now should be changed and which of his habits should be given up. At the same time he cudgeled his brains over what attributes and habits were to be substituted for those that were to be eliminated, since he had no wish to be facing another void. It had been a long time since he had given any thought to the desirable qualities of a good teacher. Either the question had not occurred to him, or in ambitious moments he had simply classified himself as a good teacher. He could not remember how he had envisaged the ideal teacher in his student days. He could not even remember whether he had ever had such an ideal.

To avoid the risk of recognizing the characteristics of a good teacher in a superficial way, and quickly forgetting them again in complacency over the mere feat of recognition, he took a sheet of paper. On the point of starting to write, he was struck by the thought that he might do well to talk to other teachers first, or, if not with teachers, with other people. Then he told himself that he was concerned only with the opinion of that particular teacher who at this time was himself. He picked up his pencil again but felt distracted by the desire for a woman, who must not be Ruth. For a few minutes he abandoned himself to this desire; then he thought: When a number of problems have to be solved at the same time, as is now the case with me, the thought of one of them will always interfere with the solution of the others. Since I don't wish to condemn myself to inactivity, I must be prepared to start on my enterprise even in a distracted condition. Then, having reached this point, he forced himself to concentrate. He alternately pondered and wrote throughout the evening and part of the night.

1. My good teacher must be an ally of his students. Not as an educational subterfuge, not like a conjurer, using his pretense of being an ally for ulterior motives, but unreservedly. Based solely on the conviction that children need allies.

2. To be an ally means having the willingness to form an alliance against someone or something, be it even the mighty school. To form an alliance against senseless practices and regulations, of which there are more than enough. Not to conceal defeat from the children, but with the children to suffer openly from it. But not to yield prematurely, not to fight like a defeatist.

How can I remain calm when one child faces unpleasant consequences due to his frankness and the other benefits from parroting the right phrases?

3. In extreme cases to be prepared to take the consequences (for there might conceivably be defeats that are unacceptable). To be willing to cease being a teacher, and thereby to gain freedom of movement. But not to turn this into too trivial a currency, for everyday use.

4. He must feel responsible toward the children, more so than toward the school administration. While mindful of the truism that school exists to prepare children for life, he must not forget that the present is also the children's life. That they are not dead, waiting to be awakened to life.

5. Feigned interest is worse than frank lack of interest, since it tempts children to reveal themselves to closed ears. Imagine a blind person who has been fooled into thinking that an empty room contains listeners interested in his experiences. How he starts talking and carries on until he realizes from the absence of reaction that he has been tricked.

6. A good teacher must have good nerves. These can't be acquired by training, or by compulsion. Only love can endow him with them. (But look at some of the people they allow to become teachers.)

7. He must take a lively interest in the various talents of his students, he must want to discover them. He must not have a mental picture of a model child to which he wants to shape all others, broken and uniform.

8. There will be times when his opinions diverge from those that the curriculum requires him to present to the class. (To him, to my good teacher, this will happen time and again.) How to react? Present only the other opinion? Or only his own? Or both? Probably the only way is to explain to the class how opinions are formed: not only by judgment but also by prejudice. This is a delicate subject. He must not cripple the children with final pronouncements, he must teach them to compare and thus to doubt.

9. He must not place himself above disagreement, hence not above doubt. He will have won when the children accept him although they could reject him with impunity.

Simrock stopped writing and imagined he was with a woman. These were not sexual desires; it was the need for a human being with whom he wanted to be on intimate terms. He imagined a young woman, very beautiful, with long, shining hair. Then he read through his notes. He crossed out the figures dividing the separate paragraphs, corrected a word here and there. Then he read it through again and thought: What a lot of trouble to try to describe a good teacher by means of theories! He tore up his notes. Later he washed his face and hands in the bathroom, where a new perfume of his mother's almost took his breath away.

He had a dream. Kabitzke was an old woman and asked him sternly: How dare you tell the students in your history class that, because of some damage to the telephone network, the October Revolution was unable to spread throughout the country? Simrock defended himself with the argument: This is the way the kids wanted to hear it, and they're the ones who matter. Kabitzke lost his temper and shouted: If you insist on working with half-truths like that, the least you can do is mention the fact that the damage to the telephone service was repaired long ago. At the same time his already enormous breast swelled to such an extent that Simrock became scared and promised to mend his ways. He wished Kabitzke were a man. He went off to Leonie to have a good cry, keeping back his tears all the way. But instead of Leonie, it was Ruth lying under the table, reading a book consisting only of blank pages. She held it out to Simrock, saying there was a certain passage she didn't understand.

Simrock did not want to hurt her feelings, so he explained the author's reasons for leaving this particular page blank. His explanation seemed amazingly convincing, even to himself. As he was about to return the book to Ruth, he noticed that she was lying under the table with no clothes on.

He said: That's why you showed me the book, and Ruth said: I noticed right away you weren't wearing any pants when you came in. Simrock saw to his astonishment that Ruth was speaking the truth. He was concentrating so hard that his head ached, but all he could think of was the sentence: If she's right, she's right. He lay down beside her, and it was as though Ruth said: That's more like it.

When he awoke he seemed to go on feeling his movements, although he was now lying quite still. He could hear his mother already moving about in the kitchen, but according to his watch, it would be another half hour before she knocked at his door and told him to hurry up. In the half-light of the room he was assailed by the thought of suicide. Simrock broke out in a sweat, yet the more often he turned the word over in his mind, the less it scared him. An option like a thousand others, he told himself. What had frightened him must have been unconscious fear, it spoke more in favor of than against suicide. Then that seemed illogical. If, indeed, there were more arguments in favor than against, fear was unwarranted, for in that case suicide would be the better solution, whereas fear should be reserved for the worse one. He must weigh the pros and cons coolly and dispassionately, which was certainly easier said than done, yet it was not unreasonable to demand such an effort, possibly the last of his life, from an intelligent person. He must, he told himself, guard against impetuous suicide.

He set about sorting out the arguments, but he had been through them ad nauseam. He would have liked to find a few new points of view for this particular occasion but couldn't see a single one. The only new aspect on the entire horizon was the potential suicide itself. It would mean an end to all his troubles, but at the same time an end to hope. Which, Simrock asked himself, weigh heavier, my troubles or my hopes? Then, after having repeated the question to himself several times without seriously thinking about an answer, he suspected himself of being naïve and dishonest as he became aware that he would never take his own life, not even for the best of reasons. He got up, opened the window, and took a deep breath. He said: "Imagine me committing suicide!" He took off his pajama top and did a few knee bends, which gave him a feeling of confidence such as he hadn't had for a long time. On happening to see his smiling face in the mirror, he broke off his exercises and felt embarrassed.

His mother knocked and called out the time. Simrock made up his mind to get through his normal functions with integrity, without pretense, starting right now with the trivial. And he managed to greet his mother in the kitchen in such a way that she noticed no difference from other mornings.

As he raised his coffee cup to his mouth, he thought: It's not all that hard outwardly to drink coffee. And while he was buttering a slice of bread he thought: If she were to say something now, I could probably behave as if I were carrying on a conversation with her. As he ate his egg, after the watcher in him had separated the taste of the yolk from that of the white, he began to wonder what impression he might be making on others. He didn't want to be someone whose gloomy, long-suffering expression kept cheerful people at a distance. That's the last thing I want, he told himself, while at the same time dreading the effort of maintaining an attitude that was not his.

One Saturday in June, Simrock went to a dance hall. He well remembered the time when he had had little difficulty in persuading the most popular of the girls to come to his room, and in his opinion an ability of that kind could no more be lost than the ability to swim or ride a bike. He had already carefully looked over the only two women teachers at the school who were unmarried. One of them was stern and brusque, with students as well as staff, and one only approached her inadvertently or on matters concerning the school. Simrock thought it possible that her lack of a man and her sour disposition went hand in hand, so that eliminating one of the evils would automatically cancel out the other. However, in view of her also not being very pretty, the risk of an error seemed too great. The other unmarried teacher, Ines Wohlgemuth, was, he believed, an informer.

Simrock was shown to a table at which two soldiers were sitting. He ordered some wine, although on his way over he had intended to drink champagne. He asked himself whether he was looking for a woman or a girl. The soldiers had very young faces, flushed kids' faces, Simrock thought. As he looked at them, he found it incongruous that the same woman or the same girl might appeal both to himself and to one of the two soldiers.

The music started up at once and was so hideously loud that Simrock grimaced. He reasoned: That's the way things are here, if I don't like it I don't have to stay. Some of the men—among them one of the two soldiers—leaped up at the first beat and ran, rather than walked, to secure a particular girl. Simrock felt he could never participate in such undignified haste. He thought: But if I think it's beneath me, I'll be too late.

The remaining soldier looked annoyed; probably he hadn't reacted fast enough or didn't see a girl he wanted to rush at. Simrock smiled. Then he reminded himself that he had no woman and had come here to rectify this condition. He carefully scanned the room. Most of the customers were on the dance floor, the tables were occupied only by those left over and those customers who had arrived in couples and only wanted to dance when they really felt like it. Simrock could find no woman who stirred him. He suddenly was afraid that the stirrings that the sight of some girls had caused in him as a young man would now no longer make themselves felt.

He drank some wine and waited impatiently for the dance to end and the next one to begin. He tried to imagine how he would leap up at the first note of the next round and dash off toward the women he now intended to select. That this was bound to make him feel ridiculous counted for less than the prospect of a conquest, the first in a long time. To be honest, he told himself, I am not nearly so keen on sleeping with a woman as on having slept again with a woman. However, the idea of ending up with a woman who wanted nothing but to have slept again with a man was distasteful to him.

At intermission time, when the girls and the men were back in their respective places, Simrock saw a woman he liked the look of sitting four tables away. She seemed older than most of the girls who had come to the place alone; Simrock guessed she was about thirty. She did not seem to know the other three women at the table, since their conversation did not include her. She was fanning herself with the menu. Simrock noticed that she was not exchanging glances with anyone, also that—like many people who are embarrassed at being alone—she was trying to look occupied. He did not take his eyes off her and, suppressing his own embarrassment, sat poised to leap, until he noticed that the band had left the platform. His right leg was almost kneeling beside his chair, ready for a kind of sprinting start, without having been ordered there by Simrock. He slowly restored it to an innocuous position and saw with relief that at least the attractive woman had not noticed his preparatory measures.

The intermission lasted longer than Simrock could maintain his tension. His glance moved away from the woman more and more often, while he told himself that a marksman's accuracy was never improved by keeping the target indefinitely in his sight. He tossed the wine down his throat and hoped this would put him in the right mood.

Then, from one moment to the next, he was struck by the suspicion that all his unhappiness arose from a pitiful lack of opinion. Whenever he had been obliged to voice an opinion, he had always—he was bound to admit—chosen the one expected by the others, thus gradually losing the capacity to form his own opinions, just as a cat that is offered only dead mice gradually loses its innate skill for hunting live ones. Simrock felt himself to be experiencing a moment of simultaneous great clarity and confusion. If at this instant someone had asked him about his ideology, he would have found it impossible to answer. Instead of making the obvious response that he was a Communist, he would now have queried the basis for such a claim, except that this was the response he had always given. He felt as if he had fallen deeply and unconditionally into a creed, and as if this creed had stopped his mouth for all time, leaving him only with the choice of constantly repeating it or of exposing himself as a defector. It was this unconditional aspect that accounted for his unhappiness, a disregard for himself as an individual that for many years he had not admitted to himself. If a person forfeits all his reservations, he thought, is he not forfeiting himself? He felt angry, at Kabitzke, too, and at all those who pretended that the highest virtue was an absence of misgivings, above all of misgivings about oneself. He longed to be someone who could share in and identify with the few important matters that did exist, and not as someone whose opinion was forever predictable and hence unimportant. He wished for a closer relationship to Communism than merely a strict adherence to his country's prevailing rules, which, as at that moment seemed clear to him, could do with some improvement.

With all this he missed the start of the music. He was startled to find that the mad rush was already under way, his two soldiers already gone. Then he found the woman at her table, and he had a feeling she had glanced his way. He realized he would really have to hurry now. The woman lit a cigarette, whereupon a young man who had just approached her table and was about to ask her for a dance walked on, pretending to be on his way to somewhere else. Simrock hesitated as he stood up. He saw another man, one of the most striking in the room, stop by the woman and nonchalantly perform the mandatory bow, his eyes already on the dance floor. Simrock saw the woman smile and say something, raising her cigarette slightly as if in evidence, and he saw the handsome man pretend indifference and nod toward the other remaining woman at her table, who immediately got up and followed him. Simrock sat down again. He waited until everyone was dancing who wanted to dance and the situation had thus stabilized somewhat. Then he got up again and went over to the woman. He noticed that her hair, which from a distance had been merely brown, had a reddish sheen. He said: "May I join you for a moment?"

The woman said: "Yes?"

Now that he saw her face right in front of him, he thought: Thank God I like it close up, too. He sat down, the way one does to have a few words, and decided on an experiment: to conduct a dialogue in which the normal rules of conversation were disregarded, in which all that mattered was to communicate with precision. He felt that would help him over his embarrassment, would perhaps also embarrass the woman a little, or at least arouse her curiosity.

He said: "I'd like to know you, but I would be glad if that were possible without having to dance."

The woman said: "I see, so you'd be glad."

Simrock could understand why her voice held a mocking note. He wished he could return to his table and rehearse the dialogue mentally. He said: "I imagine that, just as I have come here to meet a woman, you are here to meet a man."

He was curious whether this attractive woman would respond to his tone. He would of course have been prepared to adjust to some other kind of conversation but hoped it would not be on a level too far below his own. This, as he saw it, had less to do with arrogance than with the fact that respecting people in general does not necessarily follow the same rules as liking a particular person.

The woman said: "Supposing you're right; what makes you think it is you I want to meet?"

Simrock found this reply encouraging. He replied: "I never said that, that's something that has yet to be established. It is because I saw you were alone that I am sitting here now in the hope that I can arouse your curiosity."

Behind her smile he saw a flicker of eagerness, and her eyes seemed to regard him kindly.

The woman: "Can't you imagine that a person might go to a dance simply for the pleasure of being among so many people? I am speaking of a pleasure that does not go beyond the walls of this room."

Simrock: "Yes, I can imagine that, but not easily. I would never dream of such a thing. Most of the people here are pursuing their pleasure with an earnestness I find suspect. Just look around you."

The woman appeared to be amused and looked at Simrock all the more intently. She seemed on the point of making a reply that she found humorous, but then she shook her head and remained silent, like someone anxious not to be too hasty.

Simrock: "If you would prefer me to declare my intentions later and meanwhile try to make you feel kindly disposed toward me, please say so."

The woman: "That sounds as if you had a wide range of programs at your disposal."

Simrock: "Oh no. Please don't take my words as boasting, actually they are a confession of inadequacy."

The woman laughed. She pointed out to Simrock that the chair he was sitting on was available to him for the duration of this dance only, which must soon come to an end. Simrock took this to be an invitation to come up with some further suggestion, and he asked her to join him at the bar. In reply the woman gave him a look that Simrock interpreted as: Do you realize what you're getting into? She put her cigarettes and lighter back into her handbag and walked ahead of him, around the dance floor, to the bar. Simrock looked at her legs and thought, before beginning to appraise them: My eyes are still as alert as ever, it's just talking that requires more effort.

It took two weeks for Simrock and the woman to agree that he should move in with her. It was a time of buoyancy, at some moments, Simrock thought, even of happiness. For a while he lost the feeling that a tremendous effort was needed each morning to want to live and to keep going until the evening. After school he took the streetcar past the familiar cafés en route to his new home, and his work at school seemed easier, too. In class he was under less of a strain and hence better at his job. One day Kabitzke took him aside, winked with both eyes, and murmured: "Don't tell me you've already . . ." He assumed a knowing expression and wagged his finger, but Simrock did not find him impertinent. He told himself that changes would have to be very inconspicuous to escape Kabitzke's notice. Winking back, he felt less cut off from Kabitzke than in a long while.

The apartment was a converted grocery store that smelled of vanilla. The first evening, when Simrock stood in the smaller of the two rooms, which had once been the store-room, and sniffed in puzzlement, the woman explained that at the time she had had the choice between this store and another, but that the other one had smelled even more strongly of insect powder than this one did of vanilla. Her name was Antonia, Antonia Kramm, and she was younger than Simrock had guessed, twenty-eight. That first evening she had made Turkish coffee, after exchanging her dance dress for jeans and a loose gray sweater, like a soldier who doesn't want to wear his uniform a second longer than necessary. She parried his attempts to kiss her, apparently not with the intention of putting a permanent stop to them but, rather, in an admonitory way, as if to say: Surely you can show some restraint. Although he wasn't quite sober, Simrock controlled himself and kept his hands off her. Finally, when the coffee had helped to clear his head a bit, he was able to think: She's right, one evening more or less doesn't matter.

For a while he restrained himself, arguing that it wasn't Antonia Kramm's fault that he had had to make do for so long without a woman. But then came the moment when her mouth with its white teeth seemed to him more compelling than anything else, and he made another attempt to kiss Antonia. This time she pushed him away more firmly, and Simrock was seriously offended. He felt she had put one over on him. He folded his arms and refused to talk.

Antonia said: "Among the few men I have known so far, there was not one I would have gone to bed with merely to stave off the threat of boredom. I wouldn't want to give up this habit."

Simrock found this convincing. It seemed to him that, from the ocean of possible words, Antonia had fished out the very ones that could restore him to his senses. He was about to apologize, but Antonia was being so pleasant that he found himself smiling with her. He looked at his watch and feigned surprise at how quickly the time had passed.

The following day, Sunday, they took the train out into the country around Berlin where Antonia knew of an unfrequented beach. The way in which, during the train ride, she enthused over the remoteness of the little lake aroused Simrock, and in fact she did kiss him in the water and lay naked beside him on the shore behind a bastion of elderberry bushes and ferns. So this was the first woman after Ruth, this was what the first woman after Ruth looked like.

Simrock wondered whether his delight sprang from the one real-life woman beside him, or whether it was the entirely normal result of such a situation. He wondered whether he would ever be able to forget Ruth when he was with another woman, until it occurred to him that he hadn't even been thinking of Ruth. Ruth entered his consciousness only indirectly, not as a person to whom he still felt ties, but as someone with characteristics and habits that forced him to make comparisons. Ruth usually kept her eyes open, this one keeps them closed. This one—how shall I put it? he thought—is so rapt, so floating, while Ruth had been more prosaic and cheerful and ready to talk. This one has such small teeth.

He also wondered how much he meant to this attractive woman, and whether it was a mark of distinction that she gave herself to him so soon, or whether that represented her usual practice. Then he plunged into hot contentment and thought with a final effort how foolish it was to compare the incomparable.

Almost every evening during the following two weeks, Simrock went to Antonia's apartment. He had a number of reasons for this; above all he wanted to find out whether they could have a close relationship and to lose as little time as possible over it. However, he was careful not to overdo the role of observer, for after all he was a suitor, a man not only looking for someone to revere but also wanting to be such a person himself.

His visits seemed to be as important to Antonia as to him. Simrock drew this conclusion from the tacit assumption that she would always be there and from her ill-disguised disappointment when one evening he told her that he couldn't come the next. This pleased him.

On one occasion she said: "I imagine you keep comparing me with your wife. I can understand that, though I don't like it."

Surprised, Simrock asked what made her think so.

Antonia said: "Sometimes you look at me strangely. Interested yet preoccupied."

She earned her living by typing, not as an employee but as a free lance commissioned by various people, mostly, as she put it, from artistic circles. She seemed to make enough money, but in these first two weeks Simrock did not think it right to ask for details. Besides, he did not particularly care. He was more interested in other information, and Antonia freely provided details as soon as she sensed any curiosity on his part.

Once she volunteered a sort of credo that made Simrock's hair stand on end. She claimed to have noticed years before that in their country sincerity was considered desirable only when the sincere person and his numerous superiors saw eye to eye. Since then, she said, politics had been for the birds as far as she was concerned. She had been well on the way toward becoming a textbook socialist when she was struck by this insight, and ever since she had kept strictly away from anything to do with politics. In school she had lied her way through the dogma convincingly enough to get herself into the university. Unfortunately, even in physics, which she had mistakenly assumed to be an exact science, the necessity for frequent declarations of faith had become all important. For three semesters her camouflage had been perfect; then a moment's carelessness had revealed a glimpse of her true nature. The powers that be had picked and plucked away at this exposed tip until she lost her temper and admitted her dislike of the excruciatingly boring indoctrination meetings, which had nothing to do with her physics and sapped her interest in what was genuinely important. In the very act of voicing her grievance, she had become conscious of the crucial mistake she was making, but those gloating faces had so provoked her that she had been unable to stop. A week later she was expelled from the university, although she still believed she might have made a useful physicist. Since then, physics had become just another word, and she had tried to create for herself a life of the greatest possible independence. It might be said that one of her few convictions was that people must learn to leave each other alone. In any case, she felt that the most agreeable society was the one that included enough islands of solitude, even if one didn't wish to set foot on them. To know there was a place where no one could follow was a great reassurance, she said, which in her opinion nobody should be denied. In their society, however, such islands were inaccessible to ordinary mortals, and the daily compulsion of enforced togetherness was the dismal rule.

Simrock said: "The way socialism is being practiced around us shouldn't be enough to scare off an intelligent socialist."

Antonia said: "I'm merely an intelligent human being, for I have been sufficiently scared to lose interest in the whole business. I regard my total lack of interest as the only means of protecting myself."

Simrock said: "Surely you're not so foolish as to reject electricity simply because you dislike the light from a certain lamp?"

She replied with unwonted asperity that there was no place for facetious comparisons in such serious matters, and if Simrock valued peace he had better look elsewhere for a topic of conversation. Simrock called her his little black lamb, and later in bed he said she was the most reactionary wench he'd ever lain with.

Simrock determined to keep the subject in mind, but for the time being not to mention it. He did not care to think of a relationship with Antonia in which something green could be regarded without challenge as yellow, believing as he did that opportunism in a love relationship was just as undesirable as it was in any other.

While Antonia lay sleeping beside him in the narrow bed, he found himself looking forward with missionary zeal to the idea of transforming her. He thought: There will be many things about her that I shall want to alter, and that's something to look forward to. A woman who is like a completed house, all ready to move into, is not what I'm looking for.

He woke Antonia to tell her he loved her. There was a little pause, then she stroked his cheek with the back of her hand, as if thanking him for a courtesy. After a further pause, while Simrock lay puzzling over her reticence, she said she could fully understand his situation. She could well understand, she said, that he was thoroughly fed up with the void that had grown inside him. She just wanted to warn him against being too precipitate. Simrock turned on the light and looked at her in astonishment.

She said: "I've been married, too."

She told him the story of her marriage of three years, while Simrock alternately tried to picture her husband and thought of Ruth.

Thus it was two weeks after they first met that he moved in with her, with a vanload of his belongings.

Before the start of summer vacation, Simrock submitted the following written application to the school administration.

I hereby request that I be relieved of all school duties during the summer vacation, including the period extending beyond my own vacation. It is my wish to engage during this time in manual labor in an industrial plant owned by the people.

Reasons: Twelve years of continuous teaching have caused a certain routine to develop within me. Because my mind has been fixed exclusively on maintaining the curriculum and on school matters, I fear that my perspectives may have become narrow. I may well have lost my awareness of extramural events. It is my wish to seek contact with people from walks of life other than mine, not only in order to acquire knowledge of their problems but also to refresh my feelings of solidarity. Last but not least, I am eager to ascertain the extent to which my teaching corresponds to the requirements of our reality.

I trust the foregoing makes it clear that I regard the period requested as leave of absence for purposes of furthering my education.

The qualifications I expect to derive therefrom are no less important to me than most of the knowledge I was able to acquire in earlier years in training courses and seminars.

I sincerely hope that my application will be granted and remain, in the spirit of Socialism,

Yours truly,

Karl Simrock.

Although he had not lied in a single sentence, Simrock's letter contained only half the truth. One of his motives had to be withheld from the authorities who would decide on his application, since its inclusion would have amounted to giving notice: Simrock wanted to find out whether he was physically equal to manual labor. Before deciding to present opinions to his class that differed from those demanded of him, he would be wise, he felt, to see whether or not the possible consequences would overtax his strength. It seemed conceivable—indeed, likely—that even a moderate show of independence might lead to his dismissal. To close his eyes to that, he argued, would be foolish, and he found nothing reprehensible in, so to speak, simulating the consequences in order to make sure that his plan would not eventually mean merely exchanging one torment for another. What a thorough person I am, he thought.

Antonia, who had typed the letter but knew nothing of what had led up to it, called Simrock a madman. "I find it a strange kind of mania for originality," she said, "to go out of your way to look for strenuous manual work. I know what I'm talking about—when I was at the university I was required more than once to do voluntary manual labor. When I had to load hay from a scorching-hot field onto a cart, I was so utterly horrified that I shall never forget it. And you're expecting to be stimulated."

Simrock said: "Why don't you read what's in my application, before we get into an argument?"

Antonia ignored him and went on. "Or, worse still, this may be a case of a special kind of boredom. In his search for a thrill Simrock comes up with the quaintest ideas. Other people go to Africa on safari, Simrock wants to work in a factory."

Simrock: "Read the application."

Antonia: "Behind your phrases, which sound as if they were tailored to the fancy of the recipient, there is something else. You are hiding some sort of plot, and if we'd known each other longer I'd be angry. But don't make out I'm stupid by trying to persuade me it isn't so."

Simrock told himself that Antonia lacked the stability for him to divulge his plans to her. She might too easily regard as opposition what was in fact concern, an attempt to reduce the gap between the conditions of his environment and his socialist hopes. He told Antonia that there was some truth in her suspicion, but even so, would she please stop insisting on a discussion of his motivation in all this. It had nothing to do with lack of confidence but with his own insecurity; he felt like a tightrope walker for whom the slightest distraction might spell disaster.

Antonia said: "Don't you think it quite likely that the administration is also wise to you and will become suspicious?"

Simrock gave this some thought, then firmly shook his head. He moved closer to Antonia and made her put her arms around him. Then he thought it unfair to change the subject in this way. He remembered what the phony exchange of caresses had led to with Ruth and told himself that in a love relationship, failure to communicate must be fought from the very beginning.

When they were lying in bed, the thought came to him that now he really wanted to start loving, and he confided all his plans to her. He told her about his dissatisfaction with the past and with the present, about his longing for change, and about his fear of being unable to cope with the consequences of this longing. Antonia listened attentively. When he had finished, she said nothing at first, and Simrock wondered whether he hadn't been too hasty after all. Then she said: "I can understand you. But this is all so remote to me that I can't give you any advice."

Simrock felt relieved to be rid of the burden of silence. Antonia now shared his secret and was not afraid to admit her inadequacy, and that was a relief, too. He embraced her passionately and felt closer to her than on any of the preceding days.

The application was cordially and promptly approved. At an assembly, the school principal not only informed the other teachers but also commended Simrock for his sense of solidarity with the people and for his endeavor not to lose touch with the practical world, that wellspring of life for all true Communists, as he put it. Simrock felt awkward in his sudden role of shining example, and the glances of some of his colleagues so embarrassed him that he forgot all about the relief the announcement should have prompted.

Kabitzke, seated a few chairs away, passed along a folded note: *Nice going, I'd never have expected it of you!* Simrock felt himself blushing. He was seized by a fierce desire to stand up and proclaim to all these well-wishers that he was withdrawing his application, and that he had merely wanted to demonstrate how childishly easy it was to gain recognition and be held up as an example simply by making a gesture that was open to anyone. However, bearing his plans in mind, he kept silent and tried to listen.

On the way home he thought: My silence is the best proof of my determination. He began to consider what kind of job he wanted to take. It was already clear to him that not one of the occupations to be considered would be to his liking, the whole idea being to find out what effect unpleasant work would have on him. He wondered whether hard physical labor were the same as unpleasant work. His next thought was: Of course unpleasant work will affect me unpleasantly. But he would not abandon the hope that something he regarded, with no personal experience, as unpleasant would eventually turn into an occupation with which a former teacher might come to terms.

Turning two street corners, he followed a pounding noise until he saw a man tearing up the street with a pneumatic drill. Another man was gathering the chunks of asphalt into a heap; both had taken off their shirts and, as Simrock came closer, looked exhausted. Their torsos and arms could not glisten with sweat, for a layer of gray dust had settled on them, and on their faces, too, making their teeth sparkle as if from the mouths of blacks. After a while they changed places. Removing the debris seemed to be easier than drilling, because the remover had a respite until the driller had loosened the next chunk from the paving. For the first time Simrock visualized how he would fall onto his bed night after night, dead beat, his limbs racked with pain; he could already imagine his stupor and hear himself cursing his decision. He thought: It doesn't necessarily have to be the most strenuous work. One of the men called out: "Move on, Dad, or we'll charge you admittance!"

Simrock murmured an apology unintelligible even to himself and resumed his way home. When he had gone far enough for the workmen not to see him, he opened his brief-case to check whether it would hold a Thermos, a towel, a sandwich box, and an extra pair of pants. His shirt was sticking to his back; he crossed over to the shady side of the street and felt as if he had made his first contact with manual labor. At home, he asked Antonia to come with him the next afternoon when he went to look for a job.

As he could not tell her where he intended to go, she called him childish and said: "You can't just simply walk out of the apartment and look for a job the way you look for a taxi, regardless of what direction it's coming from. You have to have some idea."

Simrock suggested they go to an industrial area where he would inquire on the spot what chances there were for unskilled labor. To have any preconceived ideas merely meant preparing the ground for disappointments. He said: "Just to know you're waiting for me outside, even if nobody needs me, will be a help."

Antonia: "Oh, all right."

Simrock could tell from her face that she was still unconvinced. He recalled that with Ruth he could never count on her agreeing until the battle of words had been fought to the bitter end.

He told Antonia how he had suffered from Ruth's obstinacy, how he had been infected by it, and how many times in the course of their marriage each of them had adhered to a certain mode of behavior merely because they happened to have laid it down thus and not otherwise; how he had come to realize that in the final analysis the salvaging of love meant no more than the combating of obstinacy, and how the desire to follow this useful insight had gradually faded away in him. While he talked he saw Antonia nodding repeatedly, like someone recalling her own experiences.

The second plant on the following day was a bakery. The gatekeeper told Simrock the name of the man he should see, and Simrock wasted a lot of time trying to locate this man. While doing so, he twice went back to the factory gate and asked Antonia not to get impatient. Finally he was face to face with the man, a tiny, morose fellow, and he asked him whether they would employ him for a month during the summer vacation. In a manner that sounded aggressive to Simrock's ears, the man asked about his qualifications, and Simrock replied: "I teach German and history."

The man said: "Look, this isn't a kindergarten."

Simrock replied: "Do you think I came here wanting to work as a teacher in your factory?"

He handed the man the piece of paper bearing the permission of the school administration and, while the man read it, was tempted to take it back and say that he only wanted to be employed by obliging little men. The man handed back the paper and asked whether this one month was meant to prove his ability as a production worker. He seemed to be overcoming his suspiciousness yet to be still undecided whether to replace it with sympathizing or with gloating. Simrock said: "All I'm doing is looking for work, and I have all the patience in the world. But to be subjected to your kind of scrutiny is simply more trouble than it's worth."

He turned on his heel and walked across the big yard, although not sure whether in his agitation he was going in the right direction. He remembered there being another three or four factories on the same street; then it struck him as remarkable that after less than twenty minutes' separation he should so look forward to seeing someone as he now did to seeing Antonia. He heard rapid footsteps following him but did not turn around. The little man called out: "Hey you, wait a minute! There's always work to be found here, specially in the summer."

He took Simrock, who behaved as if he had to be persuaded, to an office and helped him fill out a questionnaire. In the column where type of work was to be specified he wrote down: *yard supervision/swamper*. When he entered the pay range and mentioned the possibility of improving the less-than-princely wages by doing overtime, Simrock wondered again whether he wasn't making a mistake. Apart from the smell of bread there was nothing here to attract him. Every corner seemed to hide a latent aversion ready to leap out at any newcomer. Even after the questionnaire he felt antagonistic toward the little man, and the job, consisting in all probability of carrying heavy loads and being ordered around, could hardly be to anybody's liking; what in the world, he asked himself, was he doing here? Then he thought it surely wasn't a good sign when a person kept raising the same arguments in his mind only to keep refuting them in the same way. The man said: "Sign here, Mac."

Simrock carefully read through each entry and refrained with difficulty from correcting the man's spelling mistakes. He signed the contract and noted that the man looked gratified, as if he had taken a prisoner. He joined Antonia, who complained about the long wait but immediately rejoiced with Simrock on hearing of his success. Tucked in among the factories was a quiet little café where they sat down and drank to a good future.

Simrock looked forward uneasily and with mixed feelings to starting work. There were moments when he could hardly wait to be sucked up into the bakery, which in his mind's eye had meanwhile become more exciting than it had been that morning, and the days seemed lifeless to him, like a hurdle of superfluous time. Then again he would fear that the work was going to crush him, that it would be so terrible that any price was worth paying to remain a teacher.

Once he said to Antonia: "It's as if I were being driven by an evil spirit. Hardly do I begin to feel a bit more at ease when

I start looking for new dangers. Mind you, I'd like to have done with these dangers, but who's to say there's not more discontent ahead for me?"

Antonia said: "Now you're talking. If I were you I'd go at once to the factory and cancel the contract. I'd even be prepared to pay a penalty."

But Simrock said: "No, no, we mustn't make too much of my present state of relaxation."

The last few days of school, he taught without really trying. Most of the students already had their minds on their vacations, and, even if he had wanted to, Simrock could not have got any concentrated work out of them. With the curriculum completed and the marking all done, he thought it best to spend the remaining periods in the most entertaining way possible, since he could not simply cancel them. He picked out a few books and had the class read aloud from them or did so himself, books he felt would stimulate the students' minds. But not one of the books had the power to bring the youngsters back from their daydreaming. Simrock was shocked to note how the verses and phrases bounced off the deaf ears of his students and shattered. He told himself that neither the words nor the holiday mood could be responsible for this, the youngsters' indifference must be due to something else. I have a deplorable share in this myself, he thought, for I have been teaching them to close their minds to anything unsettling.

However great was Simrock's desire to do something about it, he knew with equal certainty that—with one foot already on vacation—it was too late in the day. He was determined that, in the new school year, he would teach the students how important it was to let oneself be unsettled. He said: "You can go home now, that's all for today."

*

Then at last, on a Monday, he started work at the factory. Simrock put on his oldest clothes—a faded shirt that, under the name of work shirt, had lain for years unworn in a drawer, and a pair of old-fashioned pants. On the streetcar he noted how different the passengers were from those with whom he normally rode to work, nearly three hours later in the day. But he was too excited to go deeply into his impression; like some of the others, he opened his newspaper, hoping he looked like a worker behind it. A weary-eyed woman and a sad young man were within his line of vision to the left and right of the edges of his paper; then he wondered why he didn't want to be conspicuous, whether it was desirable to be inconspicuous, and why so many people were afraid of attracting attention. But in his unsettled mood he found it impossible to think logically, and he made up his mind to go into this at some later time. He took note of the streetcar stops, not knowing the district and wanting to stamp some of the landmarks on his mind.

While crossing the yard, at the far end of which his little man was standing talking to some other men, he stepped onto a rounded iron bar and lost his balance. In falling, he saw the handcart that must have lost the bar, then felt such acute pain in both knees that for a few seconds he could not get up. Inside his briefcase the Thermos had smashed, the iced tea trickled out and collected in a little hollow close to Simrock's face. Simrock saw the men cross the yard to help him, the little man with a grin of recognition, followed by two others, and he dragged himself to his feet before they reached him. He said: "It's OK."

The little man told the other two who it was who had so clumsily fallen flat on his face, while Simrock was relieved to find that his knees could function more or less painlessly. One of the men picked up the iron bar and threw it onto the handcart. Simrock inquired about the locker room, and the little man told him how to get there, adding that Simrock was to report to him as soon as he was ready. Simrock thought: He's already behaving as if he owned me. But as he walked off, he conceded that someone had to give him instructions before he started work.

Sitting in the locker room were a few men, who paid no attention to him. He shook the contents of his briefcase into a garbage can, except for his soaked work pants. He tried hard to look within himself for the reasons for his foul mood, rather than in the little man or the yard. To be honest, he thought he had probably expected to slide into the job in some miraculous fashion, gradually and pleasantly, in expectation, perhaps, of kindness and encouraging applause. But sliding into the job was possible only, he told himself, by getting down to work, not by thinking or feeling but by using one's hands.

All morning Simrock had to shovel coal. At first he was aware of a reassuring reserve of strength, but he was smart enough to slow down his momentum so as not to succumb to a novice's short-lived zeal. Even so it was not long before every movement of his hands required mental effort, and after half an hour he was already exhausted. After an hour the mountain of coal he was supposed to shovel into a chute had turned into a ferocious enemy that inflicted injuries on Simrock and took his breath away. For a short while Simrock felt he was not so much working as fighting. But before he had time to think about the difference and the borderline between the two, the next shovelful gobbled up his whole attention.

Long before noon he sat down in the coal dust, too tired to go for a soft drink. He was annoyed that while shoveling he had been so completely divorced from any higher intention. He was so totally caught up in the physical exertion that nothing remained of all that he had come to this yard to find.

Then he told himself: That, too, is part of the experience I am hoping for.

The little man discovered him and said: "That's no way to make friends with me, pal."

Simrock got up and set to work on the coal again, bothered for only a few seconds by the little man's having stopped to watch him. He shoveled slowly and in small quantities, once again a prisoner to his movements. He could think only of the shovel in his sore hands and of the slowly increasing number of steps he had to take for every new load as the coal chute moved farther and farther away from the coal pile, and of the faraway bliss of the lunch break. Glimpsed in a flicker of his mind's eye, Antonia hovered above the yard, waving a shadowy scarf. Simrock squared his shoulders and speeded up a bit, as if Antonia must not be allowed to know how backbreaking the work was. Each shovelful was a minor act of despair. Simrock lost all perspective and was more surprised than relieved when the coal had disappeared from the yard. He went to look for a broom and even swept the dust into the chute, then hid in a corner of the yard until noon.

In the lunchroom he attracted attention because, in the midst of people who were mostly working with flour and looked it, he was the only person black with coal dust. The grins on some of the faces as he walked through the room with his tray, and the question someone called out as to whether he was developing a new type of bread in the experimental lab, did not bother him. He told himself that he would look like a fool if he reacted to the banter that was the lot of every novice. He sat down at a table occupied by a woman and a man he recognized from the locker room and started to eat without appetite. His body had not yet settled down, his back hurt as if it had been drilled full of holes, he could not lean back. A bakery worker, he thought, wouldn't find work in a classroom easy either, but at least he wouldn't end up with a sore back.

Then it seemed crazy to spend a month trying to behave like some superior being, thereby precluding all contact and working in isolation. He affected an air of interest and looked around, smiling brightly at the few who were still paying any attention to him, as if he fully condoned their teasing, as if in their position he would have done no differently.

The man at Simrock's table asked: "How come you picked this place? Aren't there enough others?"

Simrock included him in his smile and felt he was being put to the test. He replied: "It was just a coincidence. Yours happened to be the first likely-looking factory gate on my route."

The man: "Then you're a loser."

Simrock: "Why? I like it here."

The man: "Then you're a winner."

He dropped his gaze as if his interest in Simrock were exhausted. Simrock did his best to resemble someone who really liked it here. He ate with a pretense of appetite and tried to look cheerful, until he wondered whether his cheerfulness were visible at all under the layer of coal dust.

He asked the man: "Don't they ever tip the coal automatically into the chute? I mean, isn't there any tipping mechanism on the coal truck?"

The man: "Don't worry, there'll be a pile for you every day."

Simrock: "But surely they must use vast quantities? Aren't the ovens heated around the clock?"

The man looked at Simrock quizzically, without sympathy. He shook his head, pushed aside his soup plate, and started on his dessert. A few seconds later, while Simrock was still wondering where he had gone wrong, the woman said: "The ovens here are electric."

After the lunch break, the little man ordered Simrock to go along on one of the vans to help deliver bread and pastries to the local supermarkets. First Simrock had to wash; his hands were smarting almost unbearably, skin had been seared off both his palms. He groaned as he rubbed the dirt off his face and arms. He thought that, right now, if only he had wished, he could have been lying on the beach, Antonia beside him and an ice-cold beer on his stomach. A feeling of shame, which seemed childish but which he could not overcome, inhibited him from asking the way to the first-aid room and having his hands bandaged.

The driver of the van was a young man with charming long hair. When Simrock sat down beside him and automatically held out his hand, the driver shook it so firmly that Simrock could not suppress a low scream. At first the young man attributed this to his own Herculean strength and grinned; then he saw Simrock's wounds and stammered an apology. He made Simrock tell him how he had come by these injuries, and the young man was seized by a compassion that stayed with him for the rest of the day. Simrock was not to touch a single tray of bread with those hands, in fact he had best not get out of the van at all. Simrock's protests were unconvincing. How goodhearted the working class is, he thought.

From one of the supermarkets the young man brought him some fruit juice, from another some chocolate ice cream. His name was Boris, and his dream was to see Liverpool. Just before they knocked off he said: "If you feel like it, you can spend your whole four weeks driving around with me. I could fix that."

While Simrock was waiting in the van outside the last store, he considered whether or not he could accept the offer. Eagerly he looked for reasons why he should, thinking: If my aim is to find a job that doesn't overtax my strength and I find that kind of a job, why should I refuse it? Just because it's less unpleasant than I imagined factory work would be? Besides, he reasoned, my idea of establishing good relations with working people can't possibly be better realized than by my establishing good relations with one specific worker.

Through the windshield he saw Boris returning with a nest of empty trays, and he felt drawn to this young man who, after all, would have had every right to insist on a division of labor. He thought: I'd be playing right into the hands of my evil destiny if I were to refuse his offer!

Antonia set about treating his wounds with camomile steam and a yellow ointment. Before starting she said: "It was bound to happen."

Simrock had placed his hands on the table like two decorations for valor in the face of the enemy. Antonia treated him as if he were *in extremis* and made him think of his mother in one of her few good moments. From her face it was clear that pity alone made her withhold the reproaches with which she was overflowing. Simrock wanted very much to caress her, but the ointment on his palms that had to be absorbed while uncovered restrained him. Instead, he tried to look at her in the way in which he would have caressed her.

When Antonia stuck a straw in the glass of juice so that he could drink without having to pick up the glass, he suddenly felt suffused with a sense of security, and it flashed upon him that, whatever he did, nothing could be more rewarding than happiness with a woman, and it was in this direction, he felt, that he was heading. He wondered whether Antonia was aware of what she meant to him; then he asked himself, and soon her, which was more important: to love or be loved. Antonia wanted to know what on earth made him think of such a thing at that particular moment.

Simrock said: "My question isn't as haphazard as it seems. Whenever I felt happy during the past few years I attributed it to mere externals. I used to think: How nice and warm it is in this room! Or: How lucky my watch was found! Or: It feels nice to be kissed behind the ear. Of course I realized that the room didn't get warm by itself, but I did so in passing, as it were, as if the person responsible for the heating were part of a machine existing solely for my comfort. Now I realize that the contentment I'm talking about is always associated with the deliberate actions of certain individuals. At this moment you are the cause."

Antonia said: "I think for me it would be more important to be loved."

Simrock: "I haven't quite made up my mind yet, but with me it's probably the other way around."

Antonia insisted on putting some more ointment on Simrock's hands before he went to bed. First she gave him a bath, then she helped him get into bed, pulled up the covers, and joked and played with him as if he were a small child. He lay still for a few minutes while she was busy in the next room, uncertain whether to think about her or about his first day at work. He started with one, then switched to the other, as if the order of his thoughts were of great importance. Then he felt a fatigue that seemed unreal, so infinitely more leaden was it than any fatigue he could ever remember. His last thought was that he couldn't have embraced Antonia anyway with his sticky hands, and that he must sleep with his hands palm up so as not to soil the nice clean sheets.

The next morning Antonia stuck an adhesive dressing on each palm and advised him to accept only such work as, first, wouldn't require the use of his palms and, second, would be so clean that he wouldn't have to wash his hands afterward. Simrock said that in the bakery that was the only kind of work there was.

As it turned out, he spent the whole four weeks helping to deliver pastries and bread. Boris, as good as his word, had spoken to the people in charge and, since they had been promising him a helper for some time, encountered no difficulty. The only objection came from the little man, who, at the sight of Simrock sitting beside Boris again, stopped the van and gruffly asked what Simrock was thinking of, picking and choosing jobs to suit himself. Boris told him to ask Schirrmeister and to keep his filthy hands off the shiny hood, or he'd have to run him down, and that really wasn't part of his job. Simrock was embarrassed by the scene yet felt gratified when all the little man could do was look angry. As they drove across town, Boris cited one instance after another of the little man's need to assert himself.

Simrock very soon discovered that there was no latent beauty in the job he had wound up in. Every day he had to revise his image of manual labor, known to him only from movies, books, and newspapers, rather than personal experience. He had assumed the greatest danger to be overexertion, but now, when that no longer threatened him on his seat in the truck, he learned to fear an enemy hitherto absent from his calculations: boredom. Stimulated by the contemporary art of his country, he had nourished the hope that, transcending the physical process, manual labor would contain an element that in some magical way would take possession of the worker, enrich his personality, and inspire him. This hope did not resemble any joyous anticipation Simrock could have defined, it was more like some inner perception that emerges only under very specific conditions; and it was not until now, when he was beginning to wonder why he was so disappointed in the job, that he recognized its presence.

True enough, he thought: x number of people are being supplied with bakery goods as a result of my work. It is equally true, though, that while I am actually carrying the trays this fact is totally irrelevant to me. Yet that is the very thing that should matter: that one's work be perceived as important and useful while in the process of being performed and not only when being thought about. A few days later, after he had picked up a certain amount of routine and no longer had to be constantly afraid of doing everything wrong, Simrock began to search for something in his work to which he could look forward. For a whole day this helped him maintain interest, for in his desire not to miss anything he did his job thoroughly and with concentration. But all he found out was which aspects seemed less tedious and which more so. The part he enjoyed most was hosing the dust and flour off the van at the end of each day's run; once Boris was holding the hose and sprayed him as wet as the van, next time Simrock did the same to him. Once, after escaping from the jet of water, spluttering with laughter and pulling his dripping shirt off his back, he realized that the van would have to be washed in the winter, too.

On asking Boris how he came to be doing this particular job, he received a surprisingly clear-cut answer. First, said Boris, he had to do some kind of job, like it or not, so why not this one; second, someone had to do this job, so why not him; third, compared with other jobs he knew it was a pretty nice one, and by now it didn't seem at all like a grind—but most likely only till he found a better one, he added.

However, once Simrock grasped that delivering bread offered him no other satisfaction than that of being able every evening to chalk up another day's work, he felt some relief, too. It was like the easing of a pressure that had weighed on him as long as he found himself in an unexplored situation. Now the circumstances were reasonably clear to him, and the remainder of the four weeks lay before him, in plain view and unappealing.

His waning interest in the job was offset by his increasing curiosity about Boris. Simrock was pleased to note that this curiosity differed from the one he had brought to the job—like the curiosity one might take along to the theater without knowing the play—and that it had arisen during the short time he had known Boris. He thought: My liking him has nothing to do with my determination to like workers.

After only a few days he was able to talk to Boris easily and naturally. In Boris's eyes, Simrock's being a teacher in normal life was no reason for either respect or condescension; he accepted this fact as an item of information that, though not without its attractive side, did not affect their joint occupation. On one occasion he said Simrock had made a mistake in taking on this vacation job: at a seaside resort he could easily have earned three times as much working as a waiter during the season. Simrock thanked him for the good advice and said he would be smarter next year. He had a feeling Boris was looking at him suspiciously, as if Boris could sense the shallow insincerity in his words but did not feel it was up to him to point it out.

Boris was a bachelor and happened, during those four weeks, to be changing girl friends, a situation that became his main topic of conversation. He had already started the new affair but not yet broken off the old one, and there was an even older one somewhere way off in the background. Simrock would not be lured into giving advice, being quick to grasp that Boris was merely pretending to be looking for it and in reality wanted to do a bit of bragging. He was glad to have run across someone more talkative than himself.

One evening he told Antonia he would like to ask Boris over. Antonia had no objection, but the more Simrock thought about it, the greater became his misgivings. He reasoned that their different interests, which in the van no doubt remained less apparent than they would at a dinner table, might easily rob their relationship of its spontaneity. He also reasoned that their relationship was basically satisfying, and that he ought not to turn something as natural as this relationship into an object of experimentation. He would have preferred Boris to invite him to his place. But since no such invitation was forthcoming, Simrock thought after two weeks that he was worrying quite unnecessarily, that he was worrying about his relationship as a swimmer panics in the middle of a lake, suddenly remembering that he has never learned to swim.

Once, on a particularly hot day, they were loading bread trays into their van, and Simrock, worn out and drenched with sweat, asked for a break. He sat down on the running board; but Boris went on loading, and when Simrock was ready to resume, he saw that the job had been finished without him. Boris waved to him to get in; Simrock looked closely at his face and found no trace of reproach in it. As they drove, he justified himself in his own eyes with the thought that Boris was used to such work, whereas he, Simrock, knew only mental toil. Then it struck him: Of course, he's fourteen years younger than I am! He didn't care for the idea that someone who was not a student but a grown man could be so much younger than himself.

On one occasion, when the van had broken down and they were waiting for the tow truck, Boris held forth on work morale. With the best will in the world, he said, there was no way a person could love *their* job. If someone claimed that shifting trays of bread from one place to another gave him satisfaction or filled him with pride, then that someone was either a liar or a fool. The best thing to do with a job like that was not to become too caught up in it, so it wouldn't get too much on your nerves. Not long ago—and this was why he was telling him all this—he had been required to sign a statement of job commitment. "And so I signed something absolutely crazy. I committed myself to exactly the kind of work they're paying me for anyway. Gertrud said I should sign, Fanny said I shouldn't, and in a way both were right. What decided me was that they would leave me in peace if I signed and wouldn't if I did not. Don't imagine that I had any other benefits in mind—there aren't any. I know some people who'll sign anything because they imagine it'll get them somewhere. That's all nonsense—obviously there are far more signatures than there are good jobs."

Simrock wondered whether in a few years Boris would be faced with decisions similar to his present ones. Then something prompted him, something he could not explain and that he later looked upon as pure habit, to demonstrate to Boris the relevance of commitment. On the one hand, he said, such commitment served as an incentive to those who did not take conscientious work for granted; on the other hand, it was a good means of providing oneself with a productive power that might be called self-generating. He pointed out the usefulness of commitment, not omitting the moral aspect: competition meant more than increased pressure for productivity; it reinforced, or perhaps even created, the sense of being part of a collective, of working for something for which others were working at the same time. Boris interrupted Simrock, who still had a great deal more to say, with the remark that, with all due respect for their friendship, Simrock could kiss his ass. Instantly Simrock felt that everything he had said, and still had in mind to say, was irrelevant.

*

During the second month of school vacation, Antonia and Simrock went on a trip to Hungary. The preparations were entirely in Antonia's hands; it was she who had planned the trip and talked Simrock into it. She maintained that until two people had traveled together, they didn't know each other properly, and at some point Simrock gave in. He had never heard her put a case so ardently; there was an eagerness about her that suggested some hitherto unknown aspect of her nature.

As Antonia intensified her pressure, he himself began to look for arguments in favor of the trip, not wanting to quarrel with her while at the same time not wanting to travel all the way to Hungary against his better judgment. He assembled a number of reasons, telling himself, for instance, that a trip might gradually wipe out the memory of four weeks' manual labor; or that a good time abroad should put him into the right mood for the battles facing him when school reopened. But the moment at which he found himself most prepared to give up his resistance coincided with the question: Why shouldn't I spend a holiday in Hungary with a woman I love and to whom it means a great deal?

Some friends of Antonia's had found a room for them in a little place said to be within walking distance of Lake Balaton. They reached their destination in the middle of the night, by train from Budapest. Simrock awoke Antonia and had to coax her to get off the train before it moved on. He would have preferred to give in to tiredness, too, and it was a miracle they did not lose any of their luggage. Their landlady was wearing a nightgown of coarse cotton; she received them—so it seemed to Simrock in his exhaustion—with businesslike cordiality, he could barely prevent her from lighting the kitchen stove and warming up something for them to eat. He fell asleep before the house had settled down again.

When he stepped out of the house next morning, after his first good night's sleep in Hungary, he immediately felt at home in the country and was glad Antonia had been so insistent. After looking about him for a few minutes, he had the feeling of having been there before, a feeling he could only explain as a manifestation of his affinity with the place. His next thought was: All those movies and TV programs are enough to confuse people's powers of recollection. He asked his way to a bank, took his place in the line, and looked around to see whether there was anything here, too, that seemed familiar.

Before long he had been so astonished by the first incident he witnessed in Hungary that he decided to file it away in his memory as an experience. A tourist stepped up to the window to withdraw some money. He presented a special kind of check: he had deposited a certain amount in a Leipzig bank and now wished to take out the equivalent. The cashier scrutinized the check and the man's identification, then said in her droll German that the check had been issued in a different name and she was only allowed to accept checks on which the first and second signatures were identical. The man replied that he was well aware of that, the check had been issued in his wife's name, and she was in bed with a fever. He said they needed the money urgently. The cashier's eyes conveyed helplessness, and she told him sadly that, even in Hungary, regulations were regulations. The man nodded but did not budge from the window, arousing sympathy and hoping for a miracle. Then, just when Simrock and the two women ahead of him were beginning to get restive, the cashier had an inspiration: she handed the check back to the man along with a sheet of paper and a ballpoint pen and, in a low voice but loud enough for Simrock to hear, suggested he practice his wife's signature. It was obvious that the man was amazed at her suggestion and didn't think much of it, but, since there was no other way of getting his money, he went over to a desk and practiced forging a check. Before it came to Simrock's turn, the man handed the cashier his sheet of paper, which bore some ten autographs. The cashier examined each in turn, shook her head at the first, then looked undecided; Simrock could tell that she was having trouble choosing the most successful forgery. Finally, having studied the paper both close up and at a distance, she pointed to one of the signatures, and the man's expression showed that he agreed with her choice. He carefully transferred the signature to the check, almost biting off the tip of his tongue as he did so. The cashier scrutinized it again, then gave him the money, her manner now suddenly abrupt. The man hastily left the bank, as if he had to make a getaway with his loot.

Simrock found the cashier's behavior outrageous. But when he was telling Antonia about it over lunch, he was already filled with regret that, in *their* country, a cashier like that was unthinkable. Antonia said she had only the vaguest idea of what he was sorry about, to tell the truth she didn't understand it at all, and she asked him to explain. Simrock replied that there was a certain kind of regret that even the person feeling it could hardly understand, and to try to explain it to someone else was completely hopeless.

From where they were staying it was in fact possible to walk to Lake Balaton only in the sense that there were no marshes or other obstacles along the way, which is all that Antonia's friend could have had in mind in describing the place. The distance was eight miles; fortunately, there was a good bus connection.

They spent the first few days at the beach or tasting

various delicacies and wines in their room. Day by day it became more evident to Simrock how Antonia's prophecy was being fulfilled: how he was accepting and enjoying her presence more and more, and how the fact of their spending twenty-four hours a day together provided only contentment and never for a moment a feeling of surfeit. Once he thought: It's really true that traveling together pays off in terms of assessing a relationship. Another time, while he was applying sun-tan lotion to Antonia's back at the beach, he said to himself: I guess I can now stop wondering whether I really love her.

After a week the weather turned cool. The landlady assured them, her tone implying that she was responsible for the drop in temperature, that the cold weather was most exceptional for the time of year and would certainly not last long. She suggested a number of worthwhile places to visit, of which, since the names sounded so foreign and were so long, Simrock failed to remember a single one a few seconds later. He suggested to Antonia that they pass the time until the return of warm weather by reading, he had brought along two books and she could have first choice: Frisch's *Sketch-book*, a rarity smuggled through customs by his Heidelberg cousin, and Hermann Kant's *Impressum*. But Antonia had no wish to read either one of them, she said she hadn't flown six hundred miles to do something she could do at home without feeling she was missing something important—in other words, much better. She wouldn't mind at all, she said, if Simrock wanted to read while she had a look around the countryside. On the second cool morning Simrock took her to the bus, by now convinced that a brief separation would add a little spice to their vacation.

He spent the morning going for a walk and thinking about the reopening of school. It oppressed him not to know what to do with his class other than what he had been doing, and he was haunted by the fear that dissatisfaction would continue to dog him and that habit alone would deprive it of its horror. Seated on a bench that stood on the only hill in sight and was still damp from the night's rain, he said aloud: "My behavior will depend on situations that as of this moment are unpredictable. The only resolution I can make at the present time is: Never again will I consent to anything merely for the sake of peace."

In the restaurant he sat at a table with two elderly Hungarian ladies who took him for a West German. Simrock chuckled to himself: Must be my determined expression. They took turns heaping praise upon his supposed native land and discoursing upon the very fine impressions they had derived from their occasional visits to that country. Simrock did not disabuse them and decided to have some fun. He pretended to be a businessman from Frankfurt and tossed off a number of opinions sufficiently outrageous to elicit protests, he hoped, from the two ladies. For example, he claimed that the matter of the distribution of power in Europe had not yet been settled, not by a long shot, even in Hungary, and that as long as the use of rockets was not acceptable it was necessary to operate with money. Further, he said—in a whisper, for fear his inanities might be audible at other tables—that, having had a good look around in Hungary, he couldn't help noticing that the Jews and gypsies were already beginning to make themselves heard again, loud and clear. But the ladies looked at him wide-eyed, lost in admiration, it seemed to him, as at someone who at last had the courage to speak his mind. Simrock was shocked to find they agreed with everything he said, and only his sense of having initiated an unfair game restrained him from telling the two ladies what he thought of them.

Back in his room, he sat down by the open window, read Hermann Kant's *Impressum,* and soon found himself waiting for Antonia. In the late afternoon, when the sun broke through the clouds for a few minutes, he felt certain that at this very moment Antonia must be thinking of him, too, and looking forward to her return, determined never again to explore the country without him. His longing for her seemed disproportionate, no more than seven hours having passed since they parted; but he reasoned that the extent of a person's longing depended less on time than on love. Then he put the book aside and tried to determine whether he wasn't inclined to exaggerate, not only in his emotions but also in whatever he considered the right thing to do or not to do.

On hearing some music that seemed to be for the benefit of tourists, he went downstairs. But when he stepped out of the house, no more music was to be heard.

Antonia had not returned by nine that evening, so Simrock began to wonder if there had been an accident. He asked the landlady to go with him to the police station as an interpreter, but she made light of his fears. She voiced the obvious assumptions that Simrock had already been turning over in his mind: the train might be late, the bus might have broken down, she might have run into someone she knew. Simrock didn't even know in which direction Antonia had gone. The landlady, while translating his quaking heart into Hungarian for her husband, gave Simrock a small glass of schnapps, as well as two sleeping pills for the night. She could not recall anyone she had ever heard of disappearing without trace during the last ten years.

Simrock went to bed. In the darkness and under the influence of the sleeping pills, his fears swelled to dimensions that even he found ridiculous: Antonia was mutilated, or had succumbed to the blandishments of a Hungarian, or she hovered between life and death on an operating table. Simrock was powerless. Finally, as he watched the flickering images almost with indifference, he thought: Let this nonsense wear itself out. Just before falling asleep, he considered it likely that Antonia, heedless as a child, had traveled on and on in the unfamiliar country and now couldn't find her way back.

During the night he was awakened by some agitated whispering, which he first perceived as mere sound. He saw the landlady standing in the lighted doorway and making gestures that seemed to call for louder words; he sat up in bed and switched on the little lamp before grasping that the police were waiting for him downstairs. He couldn't find his pants right away and feared the worst; the landlady had no idea what it was about.

The police were two mustachioed men who looked like brothers and spoke no German. Simrock had to go upstairs again to get his identification. The landlady did translate his question as to what the hell was the meaning of all this and where was Antonia Kramm but, as he could clearly make out, somewhat toned it down. One of the policemen shook his head and, looking at the landlady, said Simrock was to get dressed and come along with them. He refused to give any further information, even when Simrock asked him whether this was an arrest. As Simrock went upstairs for the second time, to put on his shirt, jacket, and shoes, he could hear his landlady sobbing. Up to now she had seemed such a businesslike person that her tears surprised him.

They drove with him to a town whose name Simrock never found out. On the way, as it gradually grew lighter and the sky promised a fine day, fear mounted in him again, first for Antonia and then for himself. The policemen, one of whom drove while the other sat beside Simrock in the back, remained silent the whole way like two people who understand each other even without words. Simrock had left his watch behind. He saw a little herd of deer running away across a field, and his fears for himself suddenly seemed despicable, although he was still furious at the arrogant manner in which the police had forced him to accompany them. Again his head filled with conjectures about Antonia from which he tried to distract himself by counting milestones or smoking and asking for a light although he knew there were matches in his pocket. The only good thing about this drive, he told himself, was the end to uncertainty that must surely await him on their arrival.

He vowed to himself never again to let Antonia out of his sight for a single second while they were in Hungary, if only she were still alive.

When he saw through the windshield the spires and chimneys of a fair-sized town approaching, the policeman sitting beside him patted him a few times on his thigh, as if trying to say in his only foreign language that everything would somehow turn out all right. At Simrock's smile he looked straight ahead again, in a fixed gaze that might mean that the display of emotion embarrassed him. Simrock thought: If even the police feel sorry for me, things must be pretty bad.

In a green baroque building that had been skillfully restored and, in Simrock's opinion as they entered it, was much too good to house civil servants, an old man in uniform asked him whether he had had any inkling of Antonia's intentions. Simrock slammed his fist down on the desk and demanded to be told what was going on. He shouted: "Who do you think I am!" He lashed out at the pair of policemen who had kept him in uncertainty for two hours and asked how long this was supposed to go on. The uniformed official seemed convinced by Simrock's fury, which also settled his question. He told Simrock that some time during the preceding evening Antonia had tried to escape over the frontier into Austria.

In Simrock's mind a hole ripped open. A shudder ran in little waves from his shoulder blades down his back, and he was at a complete loss. He only came to again when the man in uniform offered him a lighted cigarette. He asked if he might speak to Antonia. The man did not reply for a long time, apparently perplexed by Simrock's question. Suddenly the little waves on Simrock's back stopped and he broke out in a sweat as it dawned on him how dangerous secret border crossings were and how, according to Western news reports, such incidents usually ended.

They crossed a big courtyard, Simrock walking beside the official, who was saluted by two approaching policemen or soldiers but did not appear to notice them. Simrock gave him a sidelong glance and suddenly felt that surely his expression would be different if anything had happened to Antonia.

Then, while left to wait outside a closed door, he felt betrayed by Antonia. He thought: Duplicity is not too big a word. Surely her escape had been no chance decision, Antonia must have been living with it even in Berlin, even as they lay in each other's arms; it must have been Antonia's sole reason for wanting to go to Hungary. Why has she involved me in her scheming? What cause have I given her to humiliate me like this? Why did she exclude me from such a vital decision? Didn't she trust me? I can't believe that. No respect, then—what else? How could she be sure that my arguments were so insignificant that they weren't even worth listening to? Then: At least I now have a better understanding of what the newspapers mean when they write about disloyalty and betrayal. Except that newspapers have no heart and can't love.

The man in uniform poked his head through the door and told Simrock it would be a little while yet.

No, Simrock reasoned, it isn't all that easy for someone wanting to leave the country actually to try to leave. Quite apart from the risk to oneself, one makes it tough for those whose job it is to prevent escape. Furthermore, only those who leave no one behind should try to escape.

He got up, strolled along the corridor, then along another, until he realized he had lost his way in the rambling building. He had to touch four benches before finding his way back to the one that was still slightly warm from having been sat on. He sat down again and thought: I already know that I shall never forgive Antonia for last night. Apparently she's fine, apart from having been arrested. She'd better not count on my sympathy. Now she has taken the little in my life that seemed to be straightening out, and destroyed it.

Antonia, when Simrock was finally taken to see her, showed a face that bore the marks of long hours of weeping. When he entered, she raised her head only for a moment and immediately withdrew her gaze into herself again. Simrock looked at the man in uniform, as if waiting to be told what to do. The latter said something to a young man with empty shoulder boards who then reluctantly got up and left the room. The older man also went out, saying that ten minutes would be the maximum. Simrock took Antonia's hand, which was alarmingly cold and did not move, like a hand that was carefully watching what was being done to it. They were silent until Simrock began to worry about the ten minutes.

He said: "I suppose you're ashamed now."

Antonia: "I couldn't tell you before."

Simrock: "Did you know before we left home?"

Antonia: "I think so, although not in detail. But I had had it in mind for a long time."

Simrock: "And that was the only reason you wanted to go to Hungary?"

Antonia: "You mustn't put it like that. If you had been

with me, I wouldn't have tried it. The opportunity was simply too tempting. I felt I could reach out and touch the Austrian mountains."

Simrock: "Where were you, anyway? Are you sure it was the Austrian mountains? Couldn't they have been Czech?"

Antonia smiled for a moment, but immediately her face clouded over again with a sad gravity. However, she no longer hid her eyes, she looked straight at Simrock, with a hint of defiance. He noticed for the first time that there were bars on both windows.

Simrock: "Have you considered what I must be feeling like now?"

Antonia: "When you're standing at the border like that, all personal considerations go by the board."

Simrock: "I see. What's going to happen now?"

Antonia: "I'll be extradited home, and there'll be a trial. I'll be sentenced for attempted escape from the Republic."

Simrock: "For how long?"

Antonia: "I didn't ask about that before we left home."

Simrock: "Why did you have to deprive us of these few days?"

Antonia: "Don't. When I suddenly saw the border right there in front of me, it went through my mind that they probably wouldn't be so quick to shoot here. And I was right about that, no one did try to shoot me. They just ran after me, and if I could've run just a little bit faster I'd have made it."

Later Simrock had to declare that Antonia had not divulged her plan to him. His words sounded to him as if he were dissociating himself from her, but the man in uniform insisted on his only answering the questions put to him. While Simrock was truthfully recounting how long he had known Antonia and how they had met, it crossed his mind that his statement would play some part or other in a subsequent trial.

Around noon he was driven back, in the same car that had picked him up but this time accompanied only by the driver. He drank a whole bottle of kirsch, slept until noon next day, paid whatever the landlady asked, and flew to Berlin. At the customs inspection in Schönefeld, his Frisch *Sketchbook* was confiscated, but Simrock was too exhausted to summon much indignation.

He spent the rest of the vacation in a depressed state, not looking forward to school. He asked the same attorney who had helped Ruth and him with their divorce to inquire after Antonia's whereabouts and to conduct her defense. But the attorney, whom Simrock knew from his student days, declined. In confidence he told Simrock that, although he did not consider Antonia's action unworthy of defense, he did not wish to renounce all legal arguments and implore the judge for a minimum sentence by representing Antonia as a deluded and misguided woman, this being the only customary and admissible defense. As for the other matter, he said, that of establishing her whereabouts and the date of her trial, he would be glad to do what he could, not officially but via a woman he knew who worked in the prosecutor's office.

Simrock spent hours walking up and down in the apartment, and, surrounded as he was by so many of Antonia's belongings, he was acutely aware of her absence. For the first time he faced the fact that there was a long separation ahead, yet he was slow to give up his resistance to this certainty, as if a gradually growing realization were easier to bear than realization at a single blow. He opened Antonia's clothes closet and recalled days when she had worn the various pants and skirts. On one occasion he leafed through the stories of a fat young author which Antonia had not yet typed up, and he longed for the sound of her typewriter from the next room.

Then one day, when he was on his knees cleaning the floor of the apartment, he was seized by an overpowering rage at the circumstances that kept Antonia from him. Suddenly he was convinced that she had every right to go wherever she pleased, and just as much right to come back if the other place no longer suited her. To want to prevent her, came the burning realization, was an outrageous presumption, to be perpetrated only by those who looked upon happiness as something for which the time was not yet ripe.

In the evening, over a glass of beer at the tavern, he said to some people he didn't know: "Of course I can see that our country needs a certain number of people to ensure production and thus provide hope for the future. But wouldn't you agree that the manner in which this need is handled is alarming? Yet it isn't all that hard—at least theoretically—to come up with a solution: what we have already achieved should be displayed in such a way as to exert an irresistible attraction on the people we need. But who has ever tried to do that?"

The others at his table complained that Simrock was spoiling their evening and that they would rather discuss things they considered more relevant to their own lives. One girl said: "My, are you ever in a lousy mood! Why don't you order another beer instead of carrying on like that?"

How was it possible, Simrock asked himself on his way home, for him to find Antonia's attempted escape justified today, whereas only a short while ago he had been calling it outrageous and callous? It must be that, depending on his mood, he had been devoting his energy alternately to the two sides of the argument. Then he wondered whether this meant that his convictions were depending on mood, an idea that worried him. Finally he told himself: The irony of it all is that, while my mental acrobatics enable me to evaluate a given situation in more than one way, there isn't a thing I can do about the fact that Antonia is in prison.

The morning school reopened there was a rainbow in the sky. Students and teachers were already lined up for the salute to the flag when Simrock walked into the playground. The principal was in the act of reading an address that, although aimed at imbuing his audience with renewed energy, in fact merely wearied them; from across the playground Kabitzke made unintelligible signs to Simrock. After the assembly he told Simrock he had been instructed to have a talk with him. Simrock smiled at the thought of Kabitzke's believing that such a message could be conveyed by sign language. Kabitzke handed him an envelope and told him they would discuss the contents when classes were over.

During midday break Simrock read:

Dear Comrade Principal:

I find myself forced to lodge a complaint about one of the teachers of my son Klaus, i.e., his German teacher, Mr. Simrock. Three days before the start of summer vacation, an incident occurred that cannot be passed over in silence. The curriculum having been completed, Mr. Simrock read selections aloud to the class, to which in principle there can be no objection. But must not a conscientious and responsible educator first consider the effect of such material on his students? Be that as it may, Mr. Simrock failed to do so, otherwise the incident in question could never have taken place: Klaus came home that day and told us that Mr. Simrock had directed him to read aloud a long poem entitled "In Praise of Doubt"! Though it is true that the author of that poem is Berthold Brecht, each of us does have his weaker and stronger moments. Has Mr. Simrock never wondered why that particular poem is not included in the curriculum?

Klaus told us that the matter did not rest with the reading of the poem, but that the students were also made to analyze the poem, and that Mr. Simrock positively encouraged them to doubt. It is my opinion that he thereby greatly overstepped his authority as a teacher. My wife and I have invariably taken the greatest pains to shelter our children from doubt. We wish to bring them up to be good citizens who regard conscientious work rather than constant fault-finding as the driving force behind the evolution of Socialism. How then, we ask ourselves, are we to imbue them with revolutionary patience if one of their teachers makes doubters of them, thus robbing them of confidence in the future?

Quite frankly, I do not consider my fifteen-year-old son to be as yet firm enough in his convictions to withstand such insinuations unscathed. The first signs of intractability are already perceptible. If Mr. Simrock must insist on trying out his theories, he should do so on his own children, not on ours. My wife and I demand that he be taken to task in order to guarantee that in future no such abuses recur. Yours in the spirit of Socialism,

K. Nachtigall.

On rereading it, Simrock was amused by the expression "revolutionary patience": his own ear told him it should really be "revolutionary impatience." He asked those of his colleagues who happened to be in the staff room: "Can anyone tell me whether the expression is 'revolutionary patience' or 'revolutionary impatience'?" and all agreed that "impatience" was the right word. Smiling to himself, he read on, then wondered whether he should read the letter aloud to regale the others. But he refrained, because he suspected that to do so could, with only a modicum of ill will, be regarded as an act of defiance. He thought: If I did read the letter aloud, it would obviously be meant as an act of defiance. He threw the paper away, then retrieved it from the wastebasket in case Kabitzke wanted it back.

He went to Kabitzke, gave him the crumpled letter, and said: "Very funny."

Kabitzke said: "Sit down and tell me what you have to say."

Simrock sat down and said: "I can't think of anything."

Kabitzke said: "You're willing to accept the rebuke without comment?"

Simrock: "I'm surprised you even bothered to show me this nitwit's letter. Instead of telling him to stop bothering the school and me in particular with his goofy fantasies, the school has me on the carpet as if there were a complaint worthy of serious consideration."

Kabitzke: "Now wait a minute."

Simrock: "And what's more, I don't mind telling you that this man's son, this Klaus Nachtigall, is a particularly obnoxious individual who puts my resolve never to favor and never to discriminate against any student to a severe test. And it was no coincidence that I chose him to read 'In Praise of Doubt.' "

Kabitzke: "Even if I admit that I don't regard this letter as all that important, I do find it strange that you're regularly involved in some kind of trouble. How do you manage it?"

Simrock got up and said: "By being alive."

Kabitzke gestured dismissively, as if this were no time for verbal subtleties. He said: "So what do you want me to tell the principal?"

Simrock felt a pang of sympathy for him, then told himself that it was not because of *him* that Kabitzke was perpetually at a loss but, rather, because Kabitzke was so timid, and so ignorant of the happiness of freedom of movement. He said: "Tell him I'm being pigheaded and intend to continue being a thorn in the flesh of Mr. Nachtigall. And tell him I'd appreciate it if in future he would not bother me with similar complaints, since after all I do have some real problems."

He said goodbye and shook hands with Kabitzke, who clung to his hand for a long moment and looked him in the eye as if it were in there that Simrock was hiding the grounds for his inexplicable behavior. He said: "I can see that you are growing more and more inflexible. But I can't get to the bottom of your defiance."

Simrock said: "That doesn't matter, as long as the defiance is there."

It was six weeks before the attorney could tell Simrock where Antonia was being held. The trial was to take place within a few days, and, according to the attorney, past experience had shown that a prison sentence of about two years was to be expected. He did not think it worth Simrock's while to apply for a visitor's permit.

At home Simrock sat at the table, shattered, trying to recall events of two years before. Although he had long been used to thinking that time passed much too quickly, the few episodes from so long ago that he could still recall—Leonie breaking her leg, the unsuccessful suicide attempt of the couple next door, a vacation in the Thuringian Forest that had been ruined by quarrels—seemed depressingly remote. He pictured Antonia after those two years as an old crone and, although he knew better, pinned his hopes on the attorney's being mistaken. He knew he simply had no choice, for to believe the attorney, to expect from the future the thing that was most likely to happen, was too hopeless even to contemplate.

It was a torment not to be able to help Antonia—with

words of consolation, perhaps, or by making a sacrifice. It must be terrible for her to be cooped up in a cell, cut off from any encouragement, for a crime that in her eyes was no crime. He thought: A great hatred is sure to grow in her. And really, how can you persuade a person who isn't happy in a country that the correct thing is to remain there? That person will only stay out of fear of the risks involved in escaping; that's why we are surrounded by people who apparently fully endorse the system. Poor Antonia.

He went to bed and turned his mind to a new problem, one of which he had already been aware but which he had not yet thoroughly examined. He imagined a kindly fate bringing Antonia's imprisonment to an end tomorrow, so that tomorrow Antonia would walk through the door and say she was back. Would he be able to forget that in her heart of hearts she had wanted to leave not only the country but him as well? Would he ever again see her as a woman he could blindly trust? He thought: I should not allow the injustice being done her to make me forget that I have been duped.

But then it struck him that Antonia's only reason for acting in secret might have been consideration for him, that perhaps she had not wanted to expose him to the necessity of lying, and that therefore her secrecy might have been a last act of love. This theory seemed just as likely as the previous one, and his head began to ache. Confused, he fell asleep, woke up a few times during the night, and each time tried hard to escape from his problems by falling asleep again as quickly as possible.

Next morning at breakfast, he felt annoyed with himself for constantly drifting into a mood of resignation. My threshold of despair is too low, he thought. He almost choked on his coffee when it struck him that this resignation might actually be nothing but laziness. Yet he suspected that it was no use making new resolutions as long as his attitude toward resolutions in general remained unchanged.

In class Simrock announced his intention of making a number of changes in his teaching; however, since he did not wish to make these changes over the heads of his students and thus repeat his mistakes, he was asking them all to meet in the history room after the last period so that they could put their heads together and come up with something. He had the impression that the slight stir following his offer signified assent. "But don't come just as spectators. The most welcome ones will be those who bring suggestions. And don't think I expect you to have a solution for everything. If you will simply tell me where I go wrong in my teaching, that'll be a big help."

But no one turned up. Simrock waited for twenty minutes in the hope that the teacher of the last period had overrun his time; then through the window he saw two boys from his class wrestling in the playground and knew he need wait no longer. He sat down and puzzled over the reasons behind this fiasco, but before discovering even the first of them he got up again and said aloud: "That's enough analysis."

He whistled as he walked through the school until one of his fellow teachers, who was still giving a lesson, flung open his door in irritation. In the playground the two boys were still grimly rolling around in the dust, so monotonously that even the most patient onlookers had left. Simrock wondered what was the use of a fight in which the opponents did no more to each other than remain tightly embraced, so that one would be forced to roll wherever the other rolled.

Simrock separated them. They appeared quite beside themselves, and it was obvious that, the moment he turned his back, they would fall on each other again. He allowed them a breather before asking why they hadn't responded to his invitation. They looked at each other, united for a moment in their amazement at their teacher's choosing to bring up such a matter at such a moment. Then one of them shrugged his shoulders; the other, with great presence of mind, said that, at the time when Simrock had first mentioned the subject, they had already arranged to have a fight. Simrock asked why none of the others had come, and neither of them had an answer. Simrock said: "I do understand you correctly, don't I? If you hadn't happened to agree beforehand to fight, you would have come to the history room?" The boys confirmed that vigorously.

Simrock: "But what about the others? Could it be that they believe nothing will change anyway?"

One boy: "Yes, that could be."

Simrock: "Maybe they're so satisfied with the teaching that they feel no need for a change?"

The other: "Yes, that could be, too."

Simrock asked no more. He realized he could count on any answer he wanted, both boys being anxious to get rid of him and fall upon each other again. He sought a final word but found none, so he pushed them into each other's arms like two parts of a whole that he had taken apart and now must put back together. After his first few steps across the playground, the panting behind him became audible, and, on looking back from the gate, he could see the two boys hugging each other again and toppling over and continuing their joyless fight.

As luck would have it, on the morning of the day of the trial, Simrock's alarm clock failed to go off. Simrock swore, had a hard time finding a taxi, and arrived at the courthouse an hour late. Standing outside the door of the courtroom was a policewoman who refused to let him in. Simrock asked whether all the seats in the room were taken, whereupon the policewoman pointed to a notice beside the door stating that the public was excluded from the trial of Antonia Kramm. Simrock said: "What do they mean, public—I live with her. We're as good as married."

The policewoman, who was middle-aged and impressed Simrock as being patient and prepared to compromise, smiled indulgently and said: "I'm telling you, no one's allowed in."

Reluctantly Simrock saw the futility of trying to convince her. He inquired whether there were any other exit from the courtroom than this one and, when she had said no, sat down on a bench facing the door. After sitting there for a few mintues, his eyes on the door and his mind a blank, he told himself that not to be let in might even be an advantage, for even if his curiosity, and his desire to see Antonia, remained unsatisfied, he wouldn't have to listen to the accusations made by the prosecution. In any event, he had no influence on the course of the trial, the events behind the door were prefabricated, predetermined, and tragic. Then he even doubted whether Antonia would welcome his presence: to have a witness to her plight could not be pleasant for her, and, he told himself, if she should decide to show remorse in order to reduce the sentence, he would have been only a hindrance to her as a spectator.

He asked how long the trial was likely to last. The policewoman replied at unexpectedly great length, as if she welcomed some conversation in this dreary corridor: she told him it varied tremendously and that, as true as today was Tuesday, cases of border infraction had in her experience lasted anywhere from an hour to two days. Simrock took refuge from the incipient verbal torrent by walking over to an ashtray at the end of the corridor and smoking. He thought it really quite heartless of the woman to chatter away so cheerfully, for surely his first words must have told her that it was the woman he loved who was on trial.

After a long period of waiting, the door was opened from the inside. The policewoman had to restrain Simrock, and instead of seizing him by the sleeve she stopped him with an explanation. She whispered that this was a break, for how long no one could tell, and that the break would probably be followed by the Reasons for Judgment, for which, unless the judge directed otherwise, the public would be admitted.

Two men came out to stretch their legs in the corridor; Simrock would have liked to ask them a few questions, but, not knowing who they were, he refrained.

He ignored the policewoman's whisperings and took a few steps into the courtroom, which was surprisingly small. Antonia was sitting with her back to him, deep in conversation with a man in a black gown. She was wearing a green dress that they had bought together before going to Hungary. Simrock did not dare call out to her. He also feared adverse consequences for her if he simply walked over to her. Then he thought: They needn't have worried about letting in what little of the public would fit in here.

After waiting quite a while in vain for Antonia's eyes to turn to him, he stepped into the path of the two men, causing them to stop and look up. He apologized and asked: "Is it correct that the public, or I, to be exact, may enter the courtroom to hear the Reasons for Judgment?"

The two men looked at each other, one annoyed, the other as if to say: Don't mind him. This man said: "No, that is not correct."

Simrock asked: "May I at least be told what sentence has been passed on Antonia Kramm?"

The same man said: "One year and seven months, taking into account time spent in custody awaiting trial."

Simrock thanked him and stepped aside to allow the two

men to continue on their way. His first reaction was that the sentence was a stroke of luck, seeing that it was five full months short of the anticipated two years, and a windfall like that certainly didn't come his way every day. But the very next instant he felt that a year and seven months wasn't a day shorter than two years.

He went back to the open door, skirting the outstretched arm of the policewoman, who fortunately wanted to avoid a scene. Antonia was still sitting with her back to the door, but alone now, as if deep in thought. Simrock coughed a few times, then, when this did not avail, called out her name. Antonia turned around as if electrified. She started to get up but immediately checked herself as she realized her situation. Simrock tried to give her a look that he hoped was fraught with meaning. To talk across that distance was impossible, the policewoman behind him was already hissing at him. To reassure her, Simrock took two steps back. Antonia made a small helpless gesture. Simrock considered what he would say to her if a conversation were possible. Then it struck him that what he had to say could be conveyed without words, and he began to weep. He was surprised how easy it was, no effort at all, as if he had had merely to dissolve a barrier.

While the courtroom became blurred, Simrock thought that, although this was a deliberate weeping, it came to him so easily for the very reason that the tears corresponded to his mental state. He thought: Above all, though, I am crying so she'll see I am crying.

Simrock went home and became ill. He vomited and had attacks of sweating and stomach cramps; it was two weeks before the doctor diagnosed a nervous stomach condition. Simrock was put on a diet and told to avoid excitement. On his return to school, a well-meaning colleague who was also a bit of a wag expressed the hope that Simrock's state of health did not match his appearance, and advised him, if that was really the case, to give a wide berth to the classrooms inhabited by those little monsters. Simrock studied himself carefully in the mirror and decided that, apart perhaps from a certain lackluster quality of the eyes, he looked just as usual.

At one point he asked himself why he was finding the separation from Antonia more painful than the earlier separation from Ruth. One explanation might be that the bloom was not yet off his relationship with Antonia, and that, whereas in the one case he had deliberately initiated the separation, in the other he had been its victim. But almost at once he shook his head; he could distinctly remember the torments of the first few weeks without Ruth. He told himself it was not that the first separation had been easy and the second one hard, but that the memory of the first ordeal had gradually faded. Besides, there was a world of difference between remembering the ordeal of a separation and being in it up to your neck.

He dreaded loneliness, and it was not so much the lack of a woman that scared him as the prospect of being left alone with all his thoughts. I must take care, he thought, that in my solitary state bitterness doesn't get out of hand and stifle everything else; otherwise I'll become an old curmudgeon before my time, someone no longer capable of anything but destructive criticism. If only, he thought as he watched a movie, unable to relate to the boisterous story line—if only I could find some human soul to encourage me; that would be worth a thousand good resolutions.

The trouble was, he had no friends. Since he and Ruth had split up, he had avoided the few people with whom he had been on more or less familiar terms, as if they belonged to the part of their joint property that from then on belonged to Ruth. He had never given any thought to the reasons for this withdrawal; he didn't even know whether Ruth had accepted the legacy, and he had not been with Antonia long enough to miss those earlier associations. He recalled how once, many years before, he had had the idea that mixing with too many people meant frittering away his time. Now this seemed incomprehensible; surely only those not threatened by loneliness could reach such a conclusion. But since he had never been very serious about this notion, it was not enough to account for his lack of friends. A more likely cause was that he had been too impatient to listen to trivialities, too inhibited to discuss his own problems, and too lazy to put complex thought processes into words merely for the sake of having other people notice that he was not keeping them to himself. He told himself: This probably means that I'm not really the type to make friends.

He read in the newspaper about a disastrous accident caused by a negligent motorist, and he remembered that a couple with whom he had always felt at ease lived on the street mentioned as the scene of the accident. He called them up that very day, was assured he would be most welcome, and arranged to visit them on one of the following evenings.

When he arrived, he noticed that a place had also been set for Ruth. Over supper he told his hosts about his divorce and about Antonia. He made an effort not to behave like someone who had come only to unburden himself. He described the most unpleasant things in deliberately undramatic terms. He told them that Ruth and he had presented the judge with a cooked-up story so as to obtain their divorce as quickly as possible—in other words, that they had gone to court like two actors and on the best of terms; he omitted to mention that lengthy arguments had been necessary to persuade Ruth to agree to this.

After he had been talking for a while, without paying attention to their expressions, Simrock became aware of a certain awkwardness, but not of a kind that seemed to stem from sympathy or solidarity with either him or Ruth; instead, his impression was that Dorothea and Lutz found it tiresome to have to listen to all this. He hastily finished off the chapter he had just reached, then stopped and apologized for monopolizing the conversation. He was asked: "Why don't you go on, what finally happened?"

And Simrock's reply was: "Never mind, otherwise you'll start thinking I only came to test your patience. I'm glad to say my alarm bell is still working, though this time it rang a bit late. Again, please forgive me."

He was assured how very much mistaken he was, first at length by Dorothea, then, as if to efface any seeming lack of credibility, by Lutz as well. But Simrock insisted that it was now time to be sociable, so he told a joke and asked after mutual acquaintances. He wondered, while listening with half an ear, whether he might not be doing his hosts an injustice; for apart from a vague feeling, prompted merely by his sensitivity perhaps, there was really nothing to indicate that they did not want to be bothered with his tale of woe.

Nevertheless, he did not carry on with his story. He had no desire to have to keep watching their faces, and suddenly it seemed pointless to have come here at all. He recognized that even sincere sympathy on the part of Dorothea and Lutz would have been of no help to him. He had been behaving, he thought, as if telling others about his troubles was tantamount to getting rid of them. He made an effort not to blame his hosts for this, drank liqueurs, and talked about things that even an hour earlier he would not have considered worth discussing. To his surprise he soon discovered that the genial mood he had adopted out of consideration for his hosts had ceased to be a pretense: it was now genuine.

After a while he felt relaxed and cheerful, something that would not have been possible after a serious conversation. On his way home he wondered whether a bit of distraction wasn't after all the best means of coping with one's troubles. He was so drawn by the noise surging out of the open door of a tavern that he went in and passed half the night getting drunk with some quickly acquired friends.

He spent several afternoons trying hard to obtain permission to visit the women's prison. But no matter whether he was servile or arrogant, the permit was not forthcoming. Whichever way he turned, his not being related to Antonia was raised as an obstacle. On one occasion his ear caught the words "special permit," but he could not find the courthouse official authorized to issue it. In a few instances he thought he could detect that behind the refusal to let him see Antonia lurked a guilty conscience. He simply could not swallow the fact that under no circumstances could a person visit a prisoner who was not a relative. Enraged, he told one prosecutor that the monstrous thing about bureaucrats was that they were better suited to refuse applications than to grant them, whereupon he was shown the door. Simrock finally turned for help to the attorney, who merely repeated that he could do nothing, and Simrock lashed out at him, too, claiming that domesticated attorneys must really be the lowest form of human life.

So there Simrock was, with time standing still and no notion of how to use it. He visualized a daredevil rescue of Antonia, complete with rope ladders and a pistol that was actually a cigarette lighter. Then he felt he must start taking an interest again in his daughter. He bought a toy for her, and a bunch of asters with autumn leaves, and went to his former home. However, when Ruth opened the door to him, he had the feeling that he had come more on her account than on Leonie's.

Ruth received him coolly. Forestalling any inquiry about his daughter, she told him that Leonie had gone to see a friend. She thanked him for the flowers and asked whether she could offer him anything. Simrock said he would appreciate a cup of coffee, although it was obvious that the offer had been made merely for the sake of politeness. The apartment had been rearranged; the room where they were sitting and having their coffee used to be their bedroom. Ruth tipped some cookies into a silver bowl that Simrock did not remember, then leaned back as if to await the end of the interruption in silence. Simrock told himself that Ruth's extreme coolness must mean that she was still very far from indifferent. He resolved to be as considerate as possible and not to do or say anything to provoke her displeasure, for no one was more entitled to his patience than she. He asked when she expected Leonie back, and Ruth replied that there was no way of telling.

Simrock: "If you have no objection, we could sit and chat for a while. I'm anxious to know how you've been getting along."

Ruth said: "I don't want to seem rude, but I don't feel like chatting. To be quite frank, I still find it difficult to talk calmly with you."

Simrock nodded and was silent, until he felt that he would now have either to say something or to get up and leave. He asked: "How's Leonie doing in school?"

Ruth replied: "You must have seen her last report card, and she's doing well this year, too."

Simrock: "When I last saw her she had two loose teeth. Have they come out?"

Ruth: "It's unfair of you to exploit Leonie as a topic of conversation. Please stop asking me questions that are no more than stopgaps."

Simrock: "What else are we to talk about?"

Ruth: "That's the point—we have nothing to say to each other."

For Simrock these words had a dramatic ring not suited to Ruth. He wondered whether she would derive any satisfaction from hearing about all his bad luck. But then he felt that neither his ill luck nor Ruth was an appropriate subject for such experiments. In vain he waited a few mintues for Ruth to speak, then said he must be going and would come back some other time. Ruth asked him to announce his next visit with a postcard or a phone call to her office. Simrock promised and thought: Anyone else in my place would be offended.

On the street it became clear to him that he must not regard Ruth as a means of spending his free time. He wasn't even sure whether he could persuade her to take up a new life with him. But since I have no such intention, he thought, my doubts aren't so painful. He happened to look up at her window at the very moment the shade was being lowered. For half an hour he walked up and down outside the building, but Leonie never came. He began to fear he had missed her in the darkness. When, to top it all, it began to rain, Simrock felt he was being dogged by bad luck and abandoned his post.

The teaching periods seemed to trickle through his fingers, and he could find no spot in which to insert a wedge. The curriculum was so devised that it devoured every second, and to disregard it would have meant a risk at the students' expense. Thus school day followed upon school day according to prescribed rules, and Simrock had to acknowledge that innovations such as he had in mind were to be achieved not by abolishing these rules in a single classroom, but only by changing them. He was surprised that it should have taken him so long to reach this conclusion.

At the top of his list was: The curricula must be altered in such a way as to leave scope for the teachers. He longed for a chance to follow his own ideas and not always to be merely executing the intentions of others, intentions that, although similar to his own, differed from them in some important points. He believed it was only within the scope he aspired to that the personality of a teacher—that which distinguished him from all others—could reveal itself. And only then could the climate be generated in which children would grow into true individuals and not be doomed to resemble one another the way their teachers did.

However, he saw no opportunity of winning allies, or even any interested discussion partners. If I judge the situation realistically, he thought, my only choice is to write down my ideas and hand them in to the school administration—only to be saddled before very long with a disciplinary process, and God knows how that would end.

During one of those empty evenings, when Simrock felt positively sick with helplessness, he gave further thought to the subject. He found himself suspecting that the teaching programs were so tightly crammed not merely because the authorities regarded all the contents as essential. The ballast in the programs, he thought, is there deliberately and calculated to a hair; its purpose is to prevent the very thing that to me seems so important: for teachers to find time to teach and educate students according to their own beliefs. From one glass to the next, the suspicion grew in him that there was a pretty obvious lack of confidence in his teaching personality; it was regarded as an incalculable risk, and that was why conditions had been created that would prevent its development.

Simrock began to fear that his inactivity was hardening to the point where he would soon lack the strength to snap out of it. He yearned for some signal, for some clear-cut sign that would be effective because it came from a kindred spirit, showing him that he was not alone in his longings. He thought: If only I had some allies.

On one of these days, when Simrock was already wondering whether the most sensible thing wouldn't be to resign himself to accept the present situation—which, after all, was not unbearable—without a fight, he received a registered letter. It informed him that he had been granted permission to visit his fiancée, Antonia Kramm, on December 11 in the women's prison. After he had put down the letter his first thought was: How happy I shall soon feel!

In the remaining five days, Simrock's agitation grew steadily, so that some of the uninitiated—and that meant all those with whom he was in daily contact—smiled at his preoccupation and attributed it to some event that they would doubtless soon find out about. In class he participated with half an ear, the students sometimes drawing his attention to mistakes until they also realized that Simrock was not himself. On December 10 one of the boys raised his hand, stood up from his desk, and was silent for a long time, until the encouraging nods of the others and Simrock's question as to what was going on took effect. He said that they had all noticed their teacher's absent-mindedness, and so, on behalf of the whole class, he would like to ask what the matter was and whether the class could help him in any way; he had only to tell them.

Simrock stared at his students, not because he felt they had seen through him but because the question and the offer seemed to him like a confession of love. He felt he was experiencing a great moment, and that what was happening to him during these few seconds was his second happiness within a short time, probably the greater of the two. Then he realized that he was remaining silent, as if stuck for an answer, and knew he must say something and that it must not be trite.

He said: "It's like this. I have a girl friend, someone I've known for quite a while. Even though we're not married, we are very fond of each other and we live together. To be more precise, we did live together until a few months ago, since when she has been in prison. Spare me having to tell you the whole story, it's long and confused and I hardly understand it myself. In reply to your question I will merely say that I received a letter stating that tomorrow afternoon I am to be allowed to visit her for the first time. This is what's on my mind, all the time, and that's the only reason I'm so distracted. There's really nothing you can do to help, is there?"

Immediately after his last words, even before watching for reactions, Simrock felt certain that he had done the right thing. Then he saw surprise on some faces, perplexity on others. In the back row a girl was weeping; she already looked like a woman, and he had always felt her to be incapable of much emotion. He ran his fingers through the hair of the boy still standing up front and went on with the lesson. But his success was only moderate, for the lack of concentration that had previously so afflicted him now seemed to have been passed on to many of the students.

The next day, when Simrock was even more absent-minded than the previous day, the German-literature class, in which a chapter from Heinrich Mann's *Man of Straw* was to be discussed, was canceled. Instead, the principal introduced to the class a first lieutenant in the armed forces who had agreed to answer questions. The principal expressed his thanks and proceeded to paint a graphic picture of the threats to the country that our People's Army was warding off. After a while, when there was reason to suspect that the principal intended to take up the entire period, the first lieutenant placed his wristwatch audibly on the desk. The principal broke off, as if startled into awareness. He said that, although there was a lot more one might say on the subject, he would leave the field to Comrade First Lieutenant, and, somewhat nettled, he left the classroom. With a smile the lieutenant confessed that his visit was not quite without ulterior motive, for he might be able to do his bit toward steering one or other of the students toward a career they might not yet have considered: the National People's Army. Simrock squeezed himself behind a desk and hoped his students would ask intelligent questions.

But instead the students held back, and even some encouraging words from Simrock had no effect. The lieutenant was forced into a monologue in which he described the life of the officers and noncommissioned officers as being diversified and interesting, their tasks varied, and their responsibility great. Simrock found his language stilted, until he realized that he was in no position to judge: he had not been listening at all, his entire attention having been on the students. He concentrated long enough on the lieutenant's words to find his opinion confirmed. It didn't matter, he thought, that the class hadn't asked any questions, for even if they had, the officer would have said nothing different.

Then he became absorbed in the face of the boy sitting beside him and tried to imagine it under an officer's cap, shouting orders. When the boy glanced at him and gave an embarrassed smile, Simrock sensed that the lieutenant had overdone his description of the pleasures of a soldier's life. Surely, he thought, the students must suspect that, too, and he wished they would ask questions instead of being so credulous. But nothing happened, despite the officer's repeated challenge to drive him into a corner. Then Simrock reproached himself: much of the blame for the kids' silence at such a crucial moment could be ascribed to his own teaching. Obviously this could not be wiped out in a few seconds, but perhaps he could mitigate the consequences somewhat by personally asking those questions to which the answers might provide the class with some enlightenment. He raised his hand, and the officer, doubtless seeing in Simrock's gesture an attempt to break the ice, nodded innocently in his direction.

Simrock said he had quite a few questions preying on his mind: he imagined, for instance, that everyone here would like to know how much the soldiers were paid. The officer looked at him in surprise, as if to convey that, in the effort to stimulate a discussion, it was possible to overdo things. He said evasively that naturally there were differences in pay among the various ranks and that he did not have the exact figures in his head. One girl asked him how much he earned as a first lieutenant, to which he irritably replied that that really was going too far. Again Simrock raised his hand.

He didn't quite understand, he said, why it was going too far to ask about his pay, but if the lieutenant did not wish to discuss it they had no alternative but to respect this. Now to his other questions, and he would like to suggest that he ask them one after another to allow the lieutenant to obtain a general idea and perhaps, in answering them, to cover more than one point. What interested him was: How much time off did soldiers and officers have, as compared to time off in civilian occupations? Was this time off also subject to regulations? For how long did a man have to enlist, and what were his chances, within that period of enlistment, of abandoning a military career if he had made a wrong decision? Were there restrictions to social intercourse and access to information—in other words, were members of the armed forces forbidden to associate with certain persons and to listen to or watch certain programs? What were the possibilities of resisting directives that a man might consider senseless—that is, how much importance was attached to discussion? Simrock added that in asking these questions he had no intention of discouraging his students from entering upon a military career. He simply felt that this information should be provided frankly and in plenty of time.

While speaking, he had been so occupied with his choice of words that he was hardly aware of the officer. When he came to the end, he found himself looking into a face of dismay, and he had to admit that the officer's dismay pleased him. He thought: I can well believe that nothing of the kind has ever happened to you before. But there's always a first time, somewhere.

Simrock felt like someone who had long shied away from doing a certain job and who, now that he had finally embarked upon it, found it much easier than expected. The officer stood up, and for a moment it looked as if he were about to say something that could only be said while he was on his feet. Then he left the room. Simrock noticed how carefully he closed the door behind him, as if wanting to make it abundantly clear that he was not slamming it.

For a few seconds not a word was spoken, and Simrock reasoned that the incident would remain more deeply ingrained in the students' memories the longer he allowed the silence to persist. For the benefit of the few who were looking at him, he shrugged his shoulders and got up from his seat. He walked to the front, avoided all exchange of meaningful glances, and, since it was the last period of the day anyway, sent the class home. He himself remained behind alone in the classroom for a few minutes, to be there in case the officer or the principal or both should wish to speak to him. Then he, too, left the building; there were still two hours left before Antonia.

He took a streetcar to the prison and had his lunch at a little restaurant he found close by. While he was waiting to be served, it struck him that the time would have passed more quickly if an argument with the first lieutenant had arisen. He suspected that the episode had left him so cold merely because the more important event lay ahead. Although he deliberately lingered over his lunch, he still had almost an hour to kill before his visiting time arrived. He went for a walk and, outside a nursery garden, wondered whether he could take flowers or a potted plant into the prison, but finally decided that this was probably not customary.

Briefcase and coat had to be checked; he was informed that no discussion with the prisoner on prison conditions, or matters related to the crime, was allowed. Simrock asked whether Antonia had been informed of this, too, whereupon the warder looked at him as if Simrock were making fun of him. Simrock was afraid he would find himself face to face with Antonia with no idea of what to talk about.

From two sides they simultaneously entered a room that was divided across the middle by a wire grille. Simrock just caught sight of the door being closed behind Antonia. He tried to look cheerful, and Antonia was smiling, too. She sat down at the table, on the far side of the grille, and said: "Won't you sit down?"

Simrock thought he would give a lot to be allowed to spend a whole hour with Antonia with neither wire grille nor supervision. It seemed silly to ask her for a kiss, yet at the same time he thought: Why, I wonder? Antonia said: "You look paler than I remember you."

Simrock said: "Don't forget, that was during the summer."

Antonia leaned forward and said in a very low voice: "I had to pretend you're my fiancé, otherwise you wouldn't have been allowed to visit me."

Simrock: "Of course."

Antonia: "You know, it isn't as bad as I feared at first. I'm not saying this to reassure you. There are some nice people here."

Simrock: "I didn't know whether they would let me bring you anything. Or what they do about letters. Since you didn't write me any, I thought I couldn't send you any, either."

For a moment Antonia seemed confused, but the next instant he could not remember what had made him think so.

Antonia: "They may let me out earlier. They say my behavior is good. But there's nothing definite yet."

Simrock: "As you can imagine, I think of you often. Or I should say: I long for you very much."

Antonia: "It's the same with me. But tell me about school. Has anything important been happening?"

Simrock: "Everything's fine. But tell me about yourself. How do you spend your days here?"

The uniformed woman, who was sitting in a corner looking as if only taboo words would reach her ears, said: "Please don't discuss prison conditions. You have been told about this."

Simrock said: "Sorry."

Antonia: "I'm sure you're finding it hard to look after the apartment. Does it still smell of vanilla? Or aren't you living there any more?"

Simrock: "Don't be absurd. I've been thinking we might go to Hungary again for our next vacation."

Antonia: "What nonsense you talk."

Then she suggested they look at each other for a while without speaking, and to Simrock this made sense. While they were looking at each other, he was thinking: When she's free again we must forget the whole business, and the wisest thing would be to start right now. It also passed through his mind that Antonia was entitled to some kind of compensation, and since no one else would feel responsible, it would be up to him to see that she got it. He thought: I might say that I'm not the one she has to thank for all her misfortunes. But I'm the one who loves her.

Antonia said: "By the way, I'd fully understand if you . . ."

She broke off, and when Simrock asked what it was that she would fully understand, she shyly shook her head. The wardress emerged from her corner and pointed to the clock. Antonia stuck one finger through the grille. Simrock held on to it until the wardress reminded him that their time was up.

A good two weeks later, between Christmas and New Year, Simrock was summoned to City Hall, where the district school superintendent and a frail-looking man whom he did not know, and whose name he did not catch when introduced, were waiting for him. The school superintendent began by saying she was sure Simrock knew what this was about, but Simrock prevaricated by simulating surprise and saying he hadn't the slightest idea. The superintendent seemed to accept this as confirming her assumption and told Simrock she had the following information for him. Simrock nodded in smiling impatience as if to encourage her, for he was determined to put up a bold front and not give the slightest pretext for supposing that he was plagued by remorse or a guilty conscience. On his way to City Hall he had repeated to himself a number of times, as if to fix it in his mind, that he had no guilt to admit since he was aware of none, that consequently he was entitled to regard any threat of disciplinary action as unjust and to proclaim it as such.

The superintendent went on to say that, after due

deliberation and in view of all the circumstances, it had been decided that Simrock could no longer continue as an educator of children who were to grow up to be individuals imbued with the principles of the state. The latest incident in the series of Simrock's lapses was so serious that the only solution they could see was to part company with him. One of the colleagues consulted, she said, had even referred to it as a provocation.

Simrock asked: "May I know to what incident you are referring?"

The superintendent gave him a long look, as if warning him not to try any provocation here. The man beside her smiled and whispered in her ear. Simrock saw his new shoes under the desk and imagined them to be a Christmas present. The superintendent told Simrock that, needless to say, he had a legal right to appeal—but in a tone that made it very clear how unwise such a course would be.

Various comments passed through Simrock's head: some ironical, some rude, and one objective one. But before he could make up his mind he came to the conclusion that any discussion was useless because the school superintendent facing him was a woman of fixed ideas. Only the role of the man beside her was not quite clear to him. Simrock said: "Even if I were to convince you that the accusations against me were pure fabrication, you would not be able to rescind my dismissal."

The school superintendent said: "And what is more, I would not wish to."

Simrock said: "The sad part is that the kids are losing a good teacher."

The unidentified man smiled again and placed a hand on the superintendent's arm before she had a chance to reply. Simrock decided, after having sat facing him for a little while, that he didn't look that frail after all.

As he sat in the underground restaurant beneath City Hall, he was suddenly overcome by astonishment at the speed of the whole episode, then by dismay. The most frightening part, he found, was that the dismissal—which, after all, he had included in his calculations months ago as an extreme possibility—had come so soon. Even before he had really started being the kind of teacher he wanted to be. On the very first occasion, he thought, when the preliminary stages of his plan of action had hardly begun. There was at least some pleasure in the realization that his annoyance derived from his concern not about himself but about something outside himself, something in which he wished to share. That seemed to strengthen his position, for not only did it indicate his lack of fear, it also gave him a clear conscience. The next moment he was wondering: What's the use of all these good intentions if I'm no longer allowed to perform in my field?

However, the plight of being allowed to share in something only as long as one does not try to influence it seemed inescapable. Maybe there was no escape for him. He was consoled by the thought that there was more to school than school. His stomach was hurting; he paid his bill and decided that, until his next meeting with Antonia, he must keep an eye on his drinking.

He stepped out onto the street, uncertain whether to turn left or right. When he finally decided to cross the street to buy some groceries, Kabitzke intercepted him. It wasn't that much of a coincidence, Kabitzke said, the superintendent had summoned him—as representing the school administration—to inform him of the interview with Simrock. She had just done so, and he suggested they sit down somewhere and have a chat.

Simrock asked: "What about?"

Kabitzke laughed, then said he knew of a café two blocks

farther on. Simrock could sense that Kabitzke regarded him as confused and would not readily renounce his intention of withdrawing from the whole affair as decently as possible. He did not consider their friendship close enough to warrant being used for such ends. Moreover, he realized that a person in a mood such as his present one was likely to lose his self-control.

Simrock said: "Tell me honestly: if it had been up to you, would I now still be a teacher?"

Kabitzke feigned surprise that Simrock could have even the slightest doubt. Besides, he said, one should never throw in the sponge too soon. Someday a time would come that would throw new light on the affair, someday people would be mature enough to understand that malcontents like Simrock really believed they were acting for the best. He, Kabitzke, would be the first on whom Simrock could rely, and times changed faster than some people expected.

Simrock forced a display of exaggerated relief. He said: "It really does a person good to know that there are friends like you. I intend to lodge a complaint with the Ministry. To be able to tell them that my vice principal is on my side will be a great help."

Dismay immediately flooded Kabitzke's face. Simrock debated whether he should feel curiosity or disgust at the arguments with which Kabitzke would embark on his retreat. But while Kabitzke was explaining how useless it would be to go to the Ministry, since that was where the decision had been made, Simrock noted how disgust triumphed over all curiosity. A nausea that he attributed to neither the schnapps nor his sensitive stomach was taking hold of him, and he was afraid he might have to throw up right there on the street in front of City Hall. Without even bothering to think up an excuse, he turned on his heel and walked away so fast that Kabitzke, if he had run after him, would have appeared to be chasing someone he didn't want to lose.

When Simrock awoke the following morning he told himself that, even if he hadn't been fired, he wouldn't have been going to school that day: vacation had started. This meant that his dismissal had no bearing on his daily routine. He tried to fall asleep again, and on waking for the second time he was surprised to find he had succeeded. He thought: There is no sense ignoring the fact that I have lost pretty well everything a person can lose.

But then he considered it unwise to draw any conclusions at this stage, so shortly after all the turmoil; since he wasn't a reporter, there was no call for instant reporting. He decided to spend the first day doing chores that would claim his full attention. He sewed on three buttons that had fallen off his clothing since Antonia's arrest; that took less than an hour. Next he intended to make some vegetable soup from a recipe in the cook book, but he stopped in the midst of his preparations because he suddenly felt sure he wouldn't like it. While looking through the cook book for something else that could be made from the ingredients on hand, he thought: But it is also true that my losses have helped me acquire an independence such as I have never known before.

He ate a couple of wieners in a restaurant and decided that he had got through the first morning in a manner that was not unbearable. He considered keeping a diary but immediately rejected the idea, even before knowing why. He quickly told himself he didn't want to be hampered by backward glances, and the sooner he found a new way to live and make a living, the sooner he would adopt new hopes and forget the old, unfulfillable ones.

*

After lunch he went for a walk along a busy street and was saddened to think that he had not been able to make a farewell speech to his students. He pictured the class after the Christmas vacation: their teacher Simrock was gone. None of his students would ever know the reasons for his disappearance, and, because of the silence of the remaining teachers, the few youngsters who had some inkling of what had been going on would eventually forget. Simrock thought: I must admit that the gap I am leaving behind is not so great as to cause lengthy regrets over my absence.

A bakery door happened to open just as he was passing, and he was assailed by the aroma of fresh bread. He slapped his forehead and thought: But this is the very thing I've provided for!

He looked at his watch and tried to remember the schedule by which he and Boris had made their deliveries. The only fixed time he could remember was that of their final daily call, at a supermarket at the north end of town. He took a taxi and, on the way, wondered whether this impetuous step was what he really wanted. He thought: Of course it's not what I want, I would much rather have remained a teacher. Nevertheless, he found himself keenly looking forward to it, and he only hoped the feeling wasn't forced and would stand up to coming events.

He went to the bakery section, where the almost empty shelves indicated that today's delivery had not yet been made. Outside the supermarket he paced up and down in the cold. After a while he was seized by the fear that Boris might meanwhile have acquired a permanent helper. His next thought was: And how about the possibility of his having an entirely different job by now—how about that?

Keeping an eye on the street, he bought a pair of gloves in a store across from the supermarket. He told the salesgirl that the gloves must be not too dressy but suitable for heavy duty. When, some minutes later, there was still no sign of Boris, he went to the manageress of the supermarket and asked whether the bread delivery had come yet. The manageress, who did not recognize him, pointed past him and said there was the van just stopping now.

Simrock's first glance told him that Boris had cut his long hair, his second that Boris had no helper. Simrock was touched that Boris kept slapping his back, couldn't get out a proper sentence, and almost hugged him. If only for this pleasure, it seemed worthwhile to have come out here and waited for him. Together they carried the bread and pastries into the stock room, Boris seeming to take Simrock's help for granted. When Simrock set down one of the trays, the manageress did recognize him and asked where he had been all this time. In Simrock's opinion, Boris had looked better with long hair, but Boris said long hair was out now. In the van it became clear that behind the short hair was a new girl friend. Simrock wondered how to describe his situation without eliciting pity, until he realized that it was unreasonable to worry about such things at this point.

As if to force a break in the innocuous chitchat, he told Boris that he wanted to go back to delivering bread, he wasn't a teacher any more. During the long pause that followed he thought the essential had been said, the rest could wait. Boris pulled over to the curb. He asked a series of questions, and Simrock supplied the information even when the question seemed unnecessary. For instance, he patiently explained how futile it would be to swallow his resentment, as Boris suggested, and have another good talk with the fellow in charge. As he spoke, he marveled at his own patience.

When Simrock began to sense that Boris had trapped himself in his own sympathy and couldn't find his way out, he suggested that this might be the time to discuss the present. Boris nodded. He listened once again to Simrock's wish to return to his job at the bakery, and then acted as if this wish coincided with his own. With an exuberance in his voice that seemed sincere, he said that Simrock's reappearance was a real break for him, he had been seriously thinking of quitting his job—not that it was so hard, but it was so lonely—and now Simrock had turned up as if by magic and all his troubles were over.

Before they could drive on they had to wipe the windows, which were all misted over. Boris wiped each pane with a little bag tightly packed with salt. Simrock pointed out that the other cars already had their lights on. Boris said: "You'll see, for the next few years we two are going to have a ball!"

One day Simrock wondered whether he was not taking himself too seriously, whether a world in which every teacher insisted as obstinately as he did on developing his own personality would not be utter chaos, and whether his stubbornness was not doing more harm than good. Whether a little self-denial would so distort him that he would have reason to fear he would no longer be himself; and whether he was not a convinced advocate of détente, and how could such détente be brought about unless the parties in question committed a degree of self-betrayal by reducing their demands.

Then he realized he was back in the maze of questions that he thought he had solved long ago: I keep putting the same spoke in my wheel simply because I can't make the effort to regard my judgments as convincing.

He envisioned a state of certainty as one of bliss. The reason for his not having reached it could only be that he had not yet acquired the right views. Then he told himself: It would be childish to believe that I could cope with my doubts simply by resolving to stop having them. But suddenly, in the midst of his longing for a firm point of view, he had a hunch that the source that continued to nourish his uncertainty was the very one from which he drew assurance.

To Boris he said: "As long as I can remember I've always been in favor of compromise. In other words, I always wanted to compromise between what I found pleasant and what I found unpleasant. This meant I was never really happy with the result. Now I've stopped all that. I tell myself that around me there are so many consistent champions of the unpleasant that I can well afford to be consistent myself. Unfortunately I already know that, in doing so, I shall constantly be plagued by doubts."

Once again he thought: But perhaps that in itself is an advantage.

One day Boris suggested that Simrock get his driver's license because he must also think of his future. It wouldn't do, he said, for Simrock to sit beside him forever and ever as an unskilled laborer, for he knew very well that what seemed quite bearable today could soon turn into a daily nightmare. He said that, even if Simrock were to go on doing exactly the same job as now but with a driver's license in his pocket, he would earn quite a bit more money. And a few days later, when Simrock had still not responded to his suggestion, Boris said: "Besides, I know somebody who wouldn't mind your being able to take over the wheel now and again."

In February, Simrock received a letter from the school superintendent asking him to come to her office. Simrock telephoned City Hall a few times to find out what she wanted, but failed to reach her. So he went, although at first he had been determined to ignore the summons. He wore his work clothes and made sure they were generously dusted with flour. The superintendent received him cordially, seemed not to be put off by his appearance, and asked how he was getting along. Simrock spread his handkerchief over a chair as he had once seen a coal delivery man do, and carefully sat down on it. He asked the superintendent if she would kindly come to the point, since he was here during his working hours, as perhaps she could see, and had very little time to spare. But she maintained her affable expression and looked at him for a long time, until he was sure she had been directed to convey some pleasant news to him.

A secretary brought two cups of coffee; then the superintendent said that in our state no one is forsaken. After things had simmered down, the comrades in charge had discussed Simrock's case repeatedly, and they had arrived at a result that was bound to bring a smile to Simrock's face. It had been decided to allow Simrock to resume his teaching, provided he confessed his error and agreed that the educational policy must not be hampered by the random and sometimes confused notions of individual teachers.

Simrock sipped his coffee and felt that once again a decision had been made for him. For one instant his heart had beaten faster at the thought, although all his experience spoke against it, that the school administration might have acknowledged they were at fault and wished to make amends. Then, before he could think of any response, he thought: Maybe this is the only way in which authorities can admit they are wrong? The superintendent asked whether he had lost the power of speech. Simrock thought: But if that's the case, it must certainly be changed.

The superintendent continued: "I can well understand that this good news comes as a surprise to you and that you need a little time. Suppose we meet again, say in a week, and continue our discussion?"

Simrock felt he had been much too optimistic in supposing that in their own way the authorities were admitting their error; there must be some other motivation, one he could not yet fathom. He tried to put himself in the place of his opponents and was not helped by the superintendent's expression, which was gradually becoming impatient. Soon the most likely explanation seemed to be that the authorities didn't want any trouble: a teacher who had been fired was a potential troublemaker, and the most effective way of defusing him was to reinstate him in the school system and—by giving him a chance to redeem himself—at the same time settle the question of guilt.

The superintendent said: "Well, Mr. Simrock?"

Simrock, who realized that this was not the time to play detective, thought that before making a reply he would have to rekindle the anger that had seized him initially. When he felt he was ready he said: "I have kept silent for so long because I assumed there was more to come. But I see that in fact you only asked me to come here in order to convey this one message to me."

The superintendent said she didn't quite understand him.

Simrock said: "How can you hope for me to apologize for an injustice done to me? How can you expect me to feel gratitude for a humiliation? And above all: How can you want a teacher who is prepared to go along with such a proposition?"

The school superintendent rose to her feet. Her face expressed no surprise, only coldness, and Simrock judged that she had herself well under control. She is behaving, he thought, as if such situations were nothing unusual for her, but he would have sworn that, behind her frosty expression, she was dumfounded. As he went down the stairs he felt annoyed that he had not turned in the doorway and said to the superintendent: "By the way, for a limited time only I am prepared to accept an apology from those responsible for my dismissal."

He noticed that he had left his handkerchief behind on the chair, but did not go back. He told himself that anyone plunging head over heels like this into an unaccustomed role simply had too many things on his mind.

Boris was waiting for him with the bread van on a nearby parking lot. He said he was half frozen and asked what had been going on at City Hall. Simrock told him. When he had finished, Boris said Simrock had been pretty stupid to go there at all. Simrock called him a smart aleck who said one thing one day and something else the next. He asked what a person in his situation was supposed to do other than repeatedly engage in dialogue. Boris said that if the answer to that were known, a lot more people surely would get themselves into the same situation.

"Even if I'd been prepared to apologize, I couldn't have done it. I'm sure my tongue would have refused to obey me."

As they drove along he began to wonder how it could have happened that, step by step and more or less unawares, he had been pushed into this situation. He believed it to be the result of circumstances beyond his control on which he could exert influence only by daring to try to alter them. But soon, the longer he reflected on the inevitability of his course of action, he began to be troubled by the fateful aspect of it, and he tried to recall the sequence. Then he told himself: What probably disgusted me most was the fact that I never resisted. I acted as though it were not up to me to rebel against regimentation and injustices. And that means: I did not believe in being responsible for myself.

His reflections were interrupted by Boris's suddenly jamming on the brakes. Simrock cautioned him not to drive so fast, but Boris asked how else they were to make up for lost time.

When they had to give way to an ambulance Simrock was

reminded of his heart, which long ago he had thought was in bad shape but which had been bearing up nicely ever since. He immediately remembered his little pain in the classroom and his great fear that Death was breathing down his neck. He thought that, if he tried to see the whole affair in a favorable light, the anxiety born at that time and on which he was still feeding might after all have been a gain.

Printed in the United States
42846LVS00002B/92